DEADLY DROP!

When the plane reached twelve thousand feet, Natalie, the instructor, pointed to a marked circular clearing in the middle of farmland. "That's the drop zone," she shouted. "You two go first, but stick close together. I'll be right behind you."

They each gave her a thumbs-up. First Joe, then Frank jumped from the open door, followed by Natalie. Joe pulled his rip cord and yelled, "Yeeehaaa!" as his parasail billowed overhead. Natalie soon did the same, but when Frank pulled his cord, the lines tangled and the parasail flapped uselessly above him.

"Frank, pull your reserve," Joe yelled as his brother whizzed by him, dropping like lead.

Frank felt around for his reserve cord, but he couldn't reach it. His harness had been yanked sideways when the main chute didn't open right. Joe watched terror-stricken as Frank struggled to reach his cord. He fell faster and faster until he was almost out of Joe's sight!

Books in THE HARDY BOYS CASEFILES™ Series

Available from ARCHWAY Paperbacks

THE HARDY BOYS

CASEFILES™

NO. 118

THE LAST LEAP

FRANKLIN W. DIXON

AN ARCHWAY PAPERBACK
Published by POCKET BOOKS
New York London Toronto Sydney Tokyo Singapore

AN ARCHWAY PAPERBACK *Original*

An Archway Paperback published by
POCKET BOOKS, a division of Simon & Schuster Inc.
1230 Avenue of the Americas, New York, NY 10020

Copyright © 1996 by Simon & Schuster Inc.
Produced by Mega-Books, Inc.

ISBN: 0-671-56118-9

First Archway Paperback printing December 1996

10 9 8 7 6 5 4 3 2 1

THE HARDY BOYS, AN ARCHWAY PAPERBACK
and colophon are registered trademarks of Simon & Schuster Inc.

THE HARDY BOYS CASEFILES is a trademark of
Simon & Schuster Inc.

Cover photograph from "The Hardy Boys" Series © 1995 Nelvana
Limited/Marathon Productions S.A. All rights reserved.

Logo design TM & © 1995 by Nelvana Limited. All rights reserved.

Printed in the U.S.A.

IL 6+

THE LAST LEAP

Chapter
1

JOE HARDY LOOKED OUT the wall of windows at the dazzling cityscape before him. He, Frank, and their dad were dining on the top floor of the seventy-five-story Epicenter Building. The restaurant boasted a truly spectacular panoramic view of the Manhattan skyline. Although it was nearly midnight, the skyscrapers still glowed with hundreds of lights, and far below was a steady stream of holiday traffic in the streets.

"I can see why they call New York the city that never sleeps," Joe said.

His older brother, Frank, stifled a yawn. "Maybe it doesn't, but I do," he said. "I'm beat."

Fenton Hardy smiled at his sons. A former NYPD detective and now a top private investigator, the older Hardy often asked Frank and Joe to help out with his cases. Taking them to dinner was his thank-you for their role in solving a tough one involving international money laundering.

"This is a real treat, Dad," Joe said as he shoveled a huge ball of linguini dripping with clam sauce into his mouth. "Fantastic food."

"Any plans for Christmas vacation?" Fenton asked Frank.

"I'm going to take it easy for a change," Frank said, pushing his dark hair off his forehead. "Do some reading, maybe work on the van."

"How about you, Joe?" Fenton said.

"Plans?" blond-haired Joe said. "Not really, Dad. I was just going to go whichever way the wind blows."

"Good," Fenton said. "You've earned it."

A commotion erupted at the far end of the restaurant. The Hardys turned to see a woman pointing excitedly out one of the windows. "Look at that!" she cried.

Several curious patrons joined her. "What on earth are they doing up there?" said a man with his napkin still tucked under his chin.

Frank rose from the table and started toward the windows. "I've got to check this out," he said.

"Hey, Frank," Joe said, eyeing his brother's half-eaten steak. "Can I take care of the rest of that?"

"Forget it, Joe," Frank said. "I'll be right back, and it had better be there."

As Frank approached the window, he could see five figures standing together on the roof of the Metrocorp Building, a block away. The building towered over those surrounding it, so that Frank could see the figures step to the ledge and look down.

"What are they doing?" asked the woman who had first noticed them.

"It's probably one of those window-washing crews," the man with the napkin said.

"Not at this hour," another patron said.

"Hey, look at that," a man cried out. "He jumped!"

There was a collective gasp as one of the figures leaped from the rooftop toward Park Avenue, more than seven hundred feet below. Halfway to the ground, a red and blue canopy popped open above the jumper, abruptly breaking his fall. He turned around the building in an arc and sailed to the ground on a side street.

The restaurant patrons watched in fascination as two more of the figures jumped and drifted to the ground under multicolored parasails. By now Joe and Fenton had joined the rest of the crowd at the windows.

"They've got to be out of their minds," someone said.

"They're BASE jumping," Frank said.

"What did you call it?" Fenton asked.

"BASE jumping," Joe said. They watched the last two figures leap into space, one right after

3

the other. The first parasail opened, carrying the jumper out over Park Avenue and around the corner to the side street where his friends were waiting.

The final jumper was following the same path, but Joe noticed that his canopy began to flutter. The diver suddenly veered back toward the Metrocorp Building. Joe could see the jumper was trying to control his direction with his body movements, which grew increasingly frantic. It became difficult to witness the scene, which Joe feared could end only one unthinkable way.

The jumper hit the building hard and, like a rag doll, plummeted to the pavement twenty stories below.

Someone screamed, and pandemonium broke out in the restaurant as everyone rushed to the windows for a look. Frank and Joe pushed their way through the crowd to the elevator, which took them to the ground floor. The brothers raced to the spot on the avenue where the jumper had fallen. They found him lying still under his yellow, orange, and blue parasail. Pulling the fabric back, Frank put two fingers to the jumper's carotid artery. "I can't feel a pulse," he said.

"Let's see if he's breathing." Joe gingerly eased off the jumper's helmet and held the visor under his nose. A small circle of vapor appeared on the glass. "Barely," Joe said.

They heard the wail of a siren growing louder

as Fenton ran up behind them. "How is he?" he asked, breathing hard.

"Just hanging in there," Joe said. He looked down at the victim's face, suddenly aware that they were about the same age. Within a couple of minutes an ambulance screeched to a halt at the curb. Frank, Joe, and their dad stepped aside and watched the paramedics go to work. A minute later a police car rolled up and two uniformed officers jumped out. They herded the Hardys, along with a growing crowd, away from the downed jumper and the paramedics.

"Let's see if we can find his friends," Frank said. He and Joe hurried around the corner to check up and down the block where the other jumpers had landed, but there was no one in sight.

"The cowards probably took off the minute they heard the sirens," Joe said.

He and Frank returned to the site of the accident just as an unmarked police car pulled up. A tall, thin black man in a long overcoat got out and quickly surveyed the scene. He shouted to the gathering crowd, "Any witnesses? Anybody see what happened?"

The Hardys came forward as Fenton told the detective what they had seen from the restaurant.

Scribbling some notes on a small pad, the man asked "What are your names, please?"

"I'm Fenton Hardy, and these are my sons, Frank and Joe."

5

The detective looked Fenton over once and said, "Would that be Detective Lieutenant Fenton Hardy of the Seventy-first Precinct?"

"That's correct."

"Please to meet you, sir." The detective smiled and extended his hand. "Sergeant Allen Williams. I'm with Midtown South." He turned to Frank and Joe. "Your father's something of a legend in the department." His expression grew grim at the sight of the young man lying on the pavement. "Anything else, Mr. Hardy?"

"Please call me Fenton. You should probably ask my boys, though. They were on the scene before I was."

Williams turned to Frank and Joe.

"We saw him and four other guys jump off the top of the Metrocorp Building," Frank said.

"Did you see where the rest of them went?" the sergeant asked.

"The side street, sir," Joe said, pointing. "They were long gone by the time we got down here. Maybe they had a driver waiting for them. It looked like a planned BASE jump."

"Enlighten me," Williams said, scribbling in his note pad.

"BASE," Frank said. "It stands for Building, Antenna, Span, and Earth. It's a trend with some skydivers. Supposedly, they get a bigger rush jumping off fixed objects than out of planes."

"They use different equipment than on normal jumps," Joe added.

"If you ask me, none of it's normal," Williams said. "Nor is it legal. Any idea what might have gone wrong here?"

Frank shook his head. "Not really. It didn't look like there was much wind, and the other chutes opened without a hitch."

"The kid's chute opened okay," Joe said. "But then it kind of collapsed on one side. He slammed into the building and fell the rest of the way."

"Hmmm. Maybe we can get something out of him when he comes around," the sergeant said. He went over to the paramedics, who were working furiously to revive the jumper. After a quick word with a medic, the detective came back shaking his head. "It doesn't look as though he's going to make it."

"So much for answers," Joe said.

Frank glanced over at the parachute that was still lying next to the jumper. "May we take a closer look?" he asked.

"Hold it," Williams said. "This is an official investigation. I can't let just anybody go poking around."

Fenton spoke up. "Frank and Joe have been around plenty of crime scenes. They know the procedures."

The sergeant paused for a moment. "If you can vouch for your boys, I guess I'm all right with them taking a quick look."

The brothers crouched down and went over

every inch of the parasail as the detective waded into the crowd and took a few brief statements from eyewitnesses.

"What do you see?" Frank asked Joe.

"Nothing suspicious," Joe answered.

Frank frowned. "I still say there was something funny about the way his chute deployed."

By now the paramedics had stopped their efforts to revive the victim and were covering him with a sheet. Joe interrupted them. "Can you wait just a second?" He and Frank studied the boy's dive harness but saw nothing out of the ordinary. Joe then pointed to an insignia on the sleeve of his jumpsuit. "What's your take on that?"

Frank knelt down for a closer look. "It's a parachuting lizard. Probably some sort of sky-diving club insignia."

Sergeant Williams called to them. "That's enough, fellas."

The paramedics covered the victim, slid the stretcher into the back of the ambulance, and shut the double doors. Frank and Joe joined their father. "See anything?" Fenton asked.

"Not really," Frank said, "although a few things don't quite add up."

Fenton drew his jacket collar up around his ears. "No sense standing out here in the cold," he said. "Let's head back to the restaurant."

"I think I lost my appetite," Joe said.

"It'll just take a minute to pay the bill, and then we'll head home," Fenton said.

As the Hardys turned to walk back to the Epicenter Building, Joe looked up with a start.

"What is it?" Frank asked.

"That yellow van," Joe said.

Frank watched as an older model van, painted bright yellow, cruised by. "Probably just rubberneckers," he said.

"With an accident like this, they come out of the woodwork," Fenton added.

Joe kept his eye on the van. "I think this is the third time it's gone by."

"Are you sure it's the same one?" Frank asked.

"It's not every day you see a twelve-year-old model like that the color of a banana," Joe said. "Maybe we could run a trace on the plates."

"Too bad we can't read them," Frank said.

"I'll catch up to it." Joe broke into a run, heading uptown after the van. "Go get the car," he shouted back over his shoulder.

Frank looked at his father, who tossed him the car keys. "Go ahead," Fenton said. "Pick me up in front of the Epicenter Building as soon as you're done."

Frank took off in the direction of the Epicenter's garage while Joe pursued the yellow van up the avenue.

The van stopped for a red light four blocks ahead, and Joe took advantage of what might be his only chance to catch up. He broke into a sprint and tore up the sidewalk, but the light changed before he could get close enough to read the license plate. A season of football may have left him in excellent shape, but his legs were burning. He knew he wasn't going to be able to keep up this pace for much more than a quarter mile.

Meanwhile, Frank got the car in record time and raced up the avenue through two yellow lights. From the car, he spotted Joe turning east onto 59th Street. Down the block, he could see the yellow van speeding away.

Joe cut the corner of the intersection and began to dart in front of a slow-moving van. He didn't see a big newspaper delivery truck start to pass the hatchback, but Frank did.

Frank's heart was in his throat as he saw that Joe was directly in the path of the accelerating truck. He tried to shout a warning, but it was too late.

Chapter
2

JOE HEARD the truck's honking horn and squealing brakes before he realized the danger he was in. He turned and saw the truck's grille in front of his nose, and the next thing he knew, his feet flew out from under him. He landed facedown on the pavement.

Frank brought the car to a skidding halt behind the delivery truck and jumped out. From where he was, all he could see were Joe's rubber-soled shoes and the bottoms of his pants sticking out from behind the truck tire. Frank ran to the front of the truck expecting the worst. What he found instead was Joe being helped to his feet by the truck driver and his companion.

"What was I supposed to do?" the driver said.

"The kid ran out in front of us. You saw it, right?" he asked his buddy, who just nodded.

"You okay?" Frank asked Joe.

"Yeah," Joe answered, feeling his knee. "Just sore." Fortunately, the truck was able to slow down before it hit Joe, which lessened the force of the impact.

The driver and his buddy headed back to their truck.

As Joe dusted himself off, Frank thought he heard him say, "Aw, shoot."

"What?" Frank asked, looking at his brother's torn pant leg.

"Aw, shoot. The van's plate." Joe spelled it out for him. "A-W C-H-U-T-E. As in parachute. It was a custom plate. My guess is, that van belongs to one of the jumpers."

Frank nodded. "Good work. But was it worth almost getting run over?"

"We can have Sergeant Williams run a check on it in the morning and maybe find out," Joe said. "Now let's go pick up Dad and head home so we can get some shut-eye."

"I was ready for that an hour ago," Frank said as they walked back to the car.

The next morning, Joe hurried into the kitchen right on Frank's heels. "Mom, do I smell waffles?" he said. "And bacon *and* sausage?"

"That's right," Laura Hardy said. "Coming up in two minutes."

Frank sat down next to his aunt Gertrude at the kitchen table and started in on his orange juice.

"Your mother and I heard about that poor boy who fell from that building last night," Aunt Gertrude said, shuddering. "How awful."

"He didn't fall; he jumped," Frank said. "And he was wearing a parachute."

"A lot of good it did him." Aunt Gertrude sniffed. "You'd never catch me making a jump like that, even with a parachute."

"Are you sure you don't want to give it a shot, Aunt Gertrude?" Joe smiled.

Just then there was a knock at the back door. Mrs. Hardy opened it, and in marched the Hardys' friend Phil Cohen, carrying a tool kit.

"Morning, everybody," he sang out. "Did I hear you're going to jump out of a plane, Aunt Gertrude?" Phil said, making himself comfortable at the table.

"Don't be silly, Philip," she replied. "We were just talking about this terrible accident the boys saw last night."

Frank and Joe told Phil what had happened the night before while everyone helped themselves to breakfast.

"By the way, Phil," Frank said, "what brings you over here so bright and early?"

"Your dad asked me to bump his RAM by another sixteen megs and add a gigabyte to his hard drive."

"What language is he speaking?" Aunt Gertrude said.

"Phil's going to make Dad's computer more powerful," Joe explained.

"Morning, Phil," Fenton said as he strolled into the kitchen. "I'm glad you could make it on such short notice. "I've been having some problems accessing databases and keeping up with my E-mail."

No sooner had Fenton sat down than the phone rang. Laura answered it, then handed it to Fenton. "He says his name is Oliver Waller."

Frank and Joe watched their father as he listened. "I'm very sorry about your boy, Mr. Waller," Fenton said, then paused. "I'd like to help, but I'm completely booked up with cases right now. I could send my sons, Frank and Joe, over, though. They're very capable investigators. To tell you the truth, they know a lot more about the subject than I do." He jotted some notes on a memo pad next to the phone. "They'll be there in an hour." He said goodbye and hung up.

"The jumper who died last night was named Kurt Waller," Fenton said. "That was his father. Sergeant Williams told him I was an eyewitness. He wants somebody to look into it."

"Aren't the cops on the case?" Frank said.

"NYPD is apparently treating it as an accident."

"And Mr. Waller doesn't agree," Joe said.

"Right. He's obviously very upset. You'll find

out more when you meet him. They live over in Ridgeway." Fenton tore the page from the memo pad and handed it to Frank, who checked the address. He figured it was about a half-hour drive.

"The kid was only seventeen," Fenton said.

"Way too young," Joe said gravely.

"You're right," Frank added, "whether it was an accident or not."

An hour later Frank and Joe pulled up behind a TV news truck in front of the Waller residence.

"Bad news sure travels fast," Frank said as they cut across a beautifully maintained yard toward the large brick house. There were several reporters and cameramen huddled around the front door. Joe squeezed past them and rang the bell.

A reporter he recognized as Janice Gainey of the tabloid TV show *The Real Deal* said, "Don't expect to get in. They're not talking to anybody."

"We'll take our chances," Frank replied.

A moment later the door opened a few inches and the face of a man about Fenton's age appeared. The newspeople pushed forward behind Frank and Joe.

"Mr. Waller, were you aware your son was involved in such a dangerous activity?" Janice Gainey shouted.

"I told you all before," the man behind the door said, "we have no comment for the press."

"Mr. Waller, we're the Hardys," Joe blurted out before the man could close the door.

Waller opened the door just long enough for Frank and Joe to slip inside, then slammed it shut behind them. "The press has been hounding us all morning," he said wearily.

After introductions were made, Frank asked, "What would you like from us, Mr. Waller?"

"Find out why our son died. The police don't seem to have the time to deal with it," he said, a trace of bitterness in his voice.

"What can you tell us about Kurt's interest in skydiving?" Frank asked.

"He came to us about a year ago asking for permission to go to jump school," Mr. Waller said. "My wife and I refused. Maybe if we'd let him go ahead, this wouldn't have happened."

"Mr. Waller, do you happen to remember the name of that jump school?" Frank said.

Mr. Waller shook his head. "He gave me an application to sign, but I handed it back without paying much attention."

"Do you mind if we have a look around Kurt's room?" Joe said.

"I don't see why not," Mr. Waller said.

He led them upstairs. On Kurt's desk sat a new computer with all the peripherals. While Frank went through stacks of papers in a file cabinet under the desk, Joe checked through the books on the wall shelves. On the third shelf down, he found two envelopes from a photo shop.

Inside the first were pictures of skydivers, some in the air, others on the ground. There were also a couple of group shots of young men in matching jumpsuits and visored helmets like the one Kurt had been wearing the night before.

"Frank," Joe said, handing the first envelope to his brother. "Take a look at these."

While Frank studied the first set of shots, Joe opened the second and spilled its contents onto the desk.

"Now here's something," Joe said as he fanned through the photos. There were shots of a radio antenna, some tall cliffs by a river, and several New York area skyscrapers, including the Metrocorp Building, where Kurt Waller had plunged to his death.

"This looks like the Palisades," Frank said over Joe's shoulder. The Palisades, one of the area's most famous land features, lined the New Jersey side of the Hudson River above the George Washington Bridge. "Here's a radio tower, which could be anywhere. But here's the Verrazano Bridge, the Chrysler Building, the World Trade Center, and the Metrocorp Building."

"All in and around New York City," Joe said. "And all pretty good bets for a BASE jump. Looks like Kurt and his buddies were scouting around for jump sites."

Frank handed Joe a picture from the other envelope. It featured several skydivers in front of a building.

Joe studied the photo closely. "It's out of focus but it looks like the sign on the building has an S-O-N at the top, then a P, and E-M-Y below. It's not much to go on. But it's something."

Frank stuffed the snapshots in his coat pocket and went downstairs with Joe. Finding Mr. Waller in the living room, they asked him for a phone book.

He pulled the yellow pages out of a drawer, and Joe flipped to the section on parachute jumping instruction. He found five schools listed: three based at County Airport, two at Ridgeway Municipal Airport, and two more at Bayport Airport.

"We'll have to check these out," Frank said, jotting down the names, addresses, and phone numbers.

Mr. Waller walked the Hardys to the front door. "Please let me know the minute you find out anything. I don't think my wife's going to rest until we understand exactly what happened."

"Don't worry, Mr. Waller," Joe said. "We'll keep in touch."

Frank and Joe let themselves out the front door and past the newspeople still clustered outside.

Joe drove while Frank checked his list of jump schools, comparing it to the background of the snapshot. There was a Johnson Jump Academy at Ridgeway Municipal, which looked like a probable match, so they headed there first.

The runway at Ridgeway Municipal ran between two rows of buildings. "I'll check out the side by the terminal," Frank said. "You take the other side."

At the far end of the row of buildings Joe came across a clean, sky blue structure. A sign across the top read The Wild Blue Yonder. He recognized the name as one they had seen in the yellow pages at the Wallers'.

Before he could go further, Joe heard Frank shout and wave from the other side of the airport. He ran back to join him. "Find anything?" he puffed.

"Right over here," Frank replied.

Joe followed his brother between two hangars. They took a few steps into the parking lot, then Frank pointed. "There," he said.

Joe looked up and didn't notice it at first, but when Frank handed him Kurt's snapshot, it was like pieces of a jigsaw puzzle falling into place. The light was different, but the sign was the same. They were standing in front of the Johnson Jump Academy, located in a corrugated metal Quonset hut wedged between two hangars.

"Bingo," Joe said. "Let's check it out."

Inside, mismatched chairs lined the walls, and a side table held a neat stack of well-worn aviation magazines. A leather-skinned man Frank judged to be in his sixties, with a few extra pounds hanging over his belt, sat with his feet propped up on the counter, his ear to the phone.

"I told you I'd get a check to you by the end of the month," the man said. "I just didn't say which month that might be." He chuckled, then grew quiet for a moment. "All right, so sue me," he said into the phone. "And good luck trying to collect." He dropped the phone into its cradle and got to his feet.

"What can I do you boys for?"

"We're thinking about taking some jump lessons," Joe said.

"You're in the right place." The older man pumped both their hands. "Spencer Johnson at your service. Why don't you fellows sign the register? We like to keep track of everybody who goes up, just to make sure they all come down. I'll be right back." He disappeared into another room.

Joe opened the hefty register to the last full page and began scanning the entries backward.

"You check the right, I'll take the left," Frank whispered.

They were already back to July before Joe spotted it. "Here we go. Kurt Waller, July eighth," he read.

"He showed up on July third and June twenty-seventh, too." Frank turned to the previous page. "He was here at least a couple of times a week before that." He turned more pages. "For months."

"Weird he would suddenly stop coming. Wonder what happened."

They heard Spencer Johnson returning. Frank quickly grabbed a pen, signed the register, and handed the pen to Joe, who did the same.

"Sorry it took so long," Johnson said, dumping a stack of papers under the counter. "I had a hard time finding these registration forms." He placed one in front of each of the Hardys, then spun the registry around to read their names. "Frank and Joe Hardy of Bayport, eh? Welcome aboard."

"Thanks. How about giving us a tour first?" Frank said.

"My pleasure." Johnson pushed through a swinging gate at the end of the counter and led the Hardys out to one of the hangars. There they found the two planes that comprised the Johnson Jump Academy fleet. "They may not be much to look at, but these babies run like a couple of tops," Johnson said. A Cessna in need of a paint job sat next to a DC3 that looked as if it might have seen action in World War II.

"You boys have any skydiving experience?" he asked.

"We had some training and did some smoke jumping in Montana a while back," Joe said. He and Frank dug into their wallets and pulled out their jump certificates.

21

Johnson barely glanced at the papers. "Good. What do you say we go right up? The Cessna's gassed and ready to go." He patted the plane's fuselage.

Frank walked all around the craft, checking its flaps and the rudder for tension, then ducked under a wing to inspect the landing gear. He came out from under the wing and dusted off his hands. "Looks good to me."

"Great," Johnson said. "Let me round up my chief mechanic and jump instructor." He shouted in the direction of the DC3. "Hey, Nat, look lively. We've got a couple of paying customers."

The Hardys were surprised when a woman only a few years older than themselves and wearing greasy overalls and a cap emerged from the far side of the larger plane.

"Meet Joe Hardy and his brother, Frank," Johnson said to her.

"I'm Natalie Hernandez." She took off her cap and shook out a mane of long dark hair. "Ready to do some jumping?"

"Nat," Johnson said, "these fellows already have their certificates."

Natalie nodded her head. "Then let's change, pack some chutes, and go flying."

While Johnson got into the Cessna and started it up, Natalie led Frank and Joe into a storeroom filled with equipment. Although everything was well worn, it was also clean and well organized.

"Nice layout," Joe said.

"I know everything looks like it's got a lot of mileage," Natalie said. "But I assure you it's all in good working order. I check out each piece of equipment myself before it goes up. My life depends on it—just as yours does."

Frank smiled. "I'm looking forward to this."

Joe wasn't sure whether his brother was referring to the prospect of skydiving or having such an attractive instructor.

Natalie handed each of them a parasail and told them to spread them out on a long table, then repack them into their containers. Although she gave them a few pointers, it was obvious from the way they handled the gear that they knew what they were doing. Then they put on jumpsuits, helmets, and goggles, strapped the parasails to their backs, and climbed aboard the Cessna.

Johnson taxied out to the runway, and when he'd been cleared for takeoff, gave it the throttle. The little plane bounced along, picking up speed. The Cessna's nose started pointing skyward, and they cleared the trees with room to spare.

"Woooeee!" Johnson shouted. "What a day to be in the air, huh? Reminds me of the old days." While Natalie stared out the window, he went on about how he flew combat missions in Vietnam.

Once they reached twelve thousand feet, Natalie pointed to a marked circular clearing in the middle of farmland. "That's the drop zone," she shouted. "You two go first, but stick close together. I'll be right behind you."

They each gave her a thumbs-up. First Joe, then Frank jumped from the open door, followed by Natalie. Joe pulled his rip cord and yelled, "Yeee-haaa!" as his parasail billowed overhead. Natalie soon did the same, but when Frank pulled his cord, the lines tangled and the parasail flapped uselessly above him.

"Frank, pull your reserve," Joe yelled as his brother whizzed by him, dropping like lead.

Frank felt around for his reserve cord, but he couldn't reach it. His harness had been yanked sideways when the main chute didn't open right.

Joe watched terror-stricken as Frank struggled to reach his cord. He fell faster and faster until he was almost out of Joe's sight!

Chapter

3

"WE'VE GOT TO DO SOMETHING!" Joe shouted to Natalie.

"I'm going after him," she shouted back. Joe watched in amazement as she unclipped her main harness and dropped away from her parasail.

Below, Frank looked up to see Natalie flying headfirst toward him like a bullet, traveling at well over 120 miles per hour. He glanced at his altimeter: 4,000 feet. He spread his arms and legs out to slow himself down. Even in this position, he knew his minimum speed was about 118, and he had only seconds left before he met with an abrupt end. Desperately he strained to reach his rip cord. Natalie pulled up next to him at 2,500 feet.

"Your harness is twisted," she shouted. "The rip cord ring is at the middle of your back."

"I can't reach it," Frank shouted back.

"Hold on," Natalie said. She drifted over to Frank, grabbed his harness, gave it a yank, then backed off. "Try it now."

Frank reached around as far as he could. This time he felt his reserve chute ring. He wrapped his fingers around it and pulled. The reserve billowed out above him with a reassuring tug, slowing him to less than twenty miles an hour.

Natalie deployed her reserve and after a few seconds steered herself in Frank's direction. "You okay?" she shouted.

Frank gave her the thumbs-up sign. The two of them drifted to earth, where they landed smoothly at the edge of the drop zone.

They had already hauled in their chutes by the time Joe touched ground. He gathered up his chute and ran over to his brother. "Nice landing. The way you were falling I was afraid we'd have to dig you out of the ground."

"You were afraid!" Frank exclaimed. "I've never experienced fear like this." He turned to Natalie. "Thanks. That was some save."

She shrugged her shoulders. *"No problema.* Spencer trained me well. Let's get a lift back to the airport." She led them to a bus waiting on a road a few hundred yards away. "Hi, Charlie," she said to the driver as they climbed aboard.

26

"Have a good jump?" the driver asked. He was the only person on the bus.

"We had a little extra excitement," Frank said. They sat down and, as the bus pulled away, Natalie took Frank's chute and examined it closely.

"I think I know what went wrong," she said after a few minutes. "One of the lines from your main chute got caught on the reserve container."

"That's probably how my harness got all twisted around," Frank said.

"I've only seen that happen once before," Natalie said. "I'm going to file a report with the manufacturer. It'll be interesting to see what they say."

Joe nodded and looked around the bus, which was as immaculate on the inside as it was outside. "This rig looks big enough for an entire football team. And brand-new, too."

"It is," Natalie said.

"I figured the Johnson Jump Academy could barely afford to stay in business, let alone buy a new bus," Frank said. "Guess I was wrong."

"No, you weren't," she said. "It belongs to the Wild Blue Yonder, the other school at Ridgeway. They let us use it when they're not too busy."

"Nothing like a little friendly competition," Joe said.

"Let's just say it's not always so friendly, okay?" Natalie turned and looked out the window. "And besides, we pay for the rides."

27

"Sorry," Joe said. "I didn't mean to pry." They rode back to the airport in silence.

While they stowed their gear in the storeroom, Joe asked Frank, "Do you think there's any connection between Kurt Waller's accident and what just happened to your chute?"

"I doubt it for two reasons. One, I packed that chute myself and there was nothing wrong with it."

"And two?" Joe said.

"BASE jumpers don't use reserves."

"Why is that?"

"By the time you realize your main isn't going to open, it's too late. You're going into the pavement. That's why BASE jumping is illegal. The sites aren't safe. It's a misdemeanor that can land you in jail with a stiff fine."

Frank hung up his jumpsuit and headed for Johnson's office. Joe followed. Natalie was busy filling out forms at the counter.

"How much do we owe you?" Joe asked Johnson.

"This one's on me, boys." Before the Hardys could protest, Johnson added, "Nat told me what happened up there. It wouldn't be right to charge you for that."

"Well, thanks to Nat, everything turned out all right," Frank said. "So we'd still like to pay."

"We thought you might be having some money problems," Joe said.

"What gave you that impression?" Johnson said with a nasty glance in Natalie's direction.

Joe looked around. "Just a wild guess."

Johnson's shoulders sagged. "Well, you guessed right. Ever since that Wild Blue outfit opened up, I've been losing customers. If something doesn't change around here, and soon, I might have to pull the plug on this operation."

"Can you tell us a little about the Wild Blue Yonder?" Frank said.

"Sorry, but I don't keep any of their brochures around to hand out," Johnson said sarcastically. "I guess now that you know about them, you'll be heading over there like everybody else."

"Spencer, please don't start that stuff again." Natalie shook her head and left the office.

Frank pulled out his wallet and counted out the fee, gingerly placing the money on the counter. "Thanks for the lesson."

"Any time," Johnson said as the Hardys left.

Outside the office, Joe observed, "He's pretty angry."

"I suppose the threat of losing his business could do that," Frank said. "What do you say we have some lunch? Something about the possibility of kissing the ground from twelve thousand feet made me really hungry."

Storm clouds were gathering, and they blocked out the sun as Frank and Joe strode toward the far end of the terminal building. A neon sign that read Drop Inn, and under it Good Eats, winked on and off in front of the diner. The interior hadn't changed much in a half century, its walls covered with old photographs of airplanes, pilots, and crew members. Most of the tables were empty, but Joe spotted Natalie alone at a booth by the window. She was reading a book propped up in front of her while eating a bowl of soup.

"Hi, Nat. Mind if we join you?" Joe called out.

Frank pulled his brother aside and said, "I think she wants to be by herself."

"She looks lonely, if you ask me," Joe said. Before Frank could protest more, Joe strode across the room and sat down at Natalie's booth. "What's the book?"

"Aeronautical engineering," she answered without looking up.

"Sounds interesting," Joe went on.

"It is if you want to design planes."

"Is that what you want to do?" Frank asked, taking a seat across from Natalie.

"I'm not sure yet." Natalie finally raised her brown eyes when the waitress appeared.

The Hardys gave the woman their lunch orders. After she left, Joe asked Natalie, "You think a lot of Spencer, don't you?"

"You bet I do. He doesn't give most people a chance to see how kindhearted and generous he can be. When my mother was sick last year, he paid the rent and made sure that my younger brother and sister had food on the table. He never asked for a dime in return. He's taught me everything I know. For all that, I owe him big-time. Sometimes, though, he makes me so mad I could . . ." Her face started to turn red. "Anyway, let's just say Spencer hasn't always done what's best for himself or his business."

"Speaking of business," Frank said, "what can you tell us about this other jump school?"

Natalie thought for a moment. "Tomcat Kritzer started the Wild Blue Yonder about a year ago."

"Tomcat?" Joe said.

"He used to fly F-Fourteens—Tomcats—for the navy. He was a real top gun. Anyway, when Kritzer was in his teens, Spencer could see he had the right stuff. He gave him hundreds of hours of free flight lessons, jumping instruction, even pulled some strings to help him get into the naval academy. When Kritzer got out of the service, Spencer made him a partner in his school. That lasted for three years, until Kritzer met a banker who was willing to put a lot of money into a new flight school. At first Spencer was really happy for Kritzer. He can be so naive. He thought the school was going to be in another part of the country. But when he found out the Wild Blue Yonder was opening on the other side of the airport, he hit the roof."

Frank and Joe exchanged glances. "How are they getting along now?" Frank said.

"They're not," Natalie said. "Spencer hasn't

talked to Kritzer since, and frankly I don't blame him. Kritzer knew exactly what he was doing."

The waitress returned with burgers, fries, and shakes for the Hardys. Natalie glanced at the clock on the wall behind the counter and gulped down what was left of her soup. "Gotta go. I promised Spencer I'd have the DC Three running again by today." She got up and headed for the door.

"See you around," Joe called after her.

As she reached for the door, a group of young men in jumpsuits burst in. One of them, who appeared to be in his early twenties, compact and muscular, blocked her way. "Hey, Nat. How are you doing?"

"None of your business, Squirrel," she said through clenched teeth. He held the door open for her, bowing as she hurried out.

"Wonder what that was about," Frank whispered.

Squirrel and his friends took the table across the aisle from Frank and Joe's booth. The tallest and thinnest of them, with an unruly mop of blond hair, said, "Did any of you see my new canopy deploy?" He didn't wait for a reply. "I was less than a thousand feet from the zone, getting pretty hairy, when I let her rip. It popped—whoosh!—smooth as silk."

"Come on," Squirrel said. "Why does everything always have to be smooth as silk with you?" The others voiced their agreement.

"I've got to live up to my name, don't I?" the thin guy said.

"Silk, I saw you hit the ground," said an Asian guy with goggles pushed up on his forehead. "Looked like another one of your patented clodhopper landings." Several members of the group snickered.

"That's it," Squirrel said. "We'll change your nickname to Clodhopper."

"Hey, that's not fair. I've been perfecting my technique," Silk said. This brought out guffaws and several catcalls.

As the laughter died down, Frank and Joe caught Squirrel's eye. "You two look familiar," Squirrel said. "Have I seen you before?" He wore a smile, but it didn't seem to be very friendly.

"I doubt it," Frank said. "We're from Bayport. Thought we'd check out the Ridgeway jumping scene."

"It's the best around," Squirrel said, turning to his friends. "Right, guys?" Everyone nodded.

"We just went up with Spencer Johnson," Joe said. This prompted a "Boo!" from someone and scowls from a couple of others.

"Forget about Johnson," Silk said. "He's all washed up."

"You've got to get yourselves over to the Wild Blue Yonder," the Asian guy added. "That's where it's really happening."

"We'll do that," Joe said. "Thanks."

33

Squirrel offered his hand to shake. "I'm Kenny McCracken, but everybody calls me Squirrel. This is Dave Shima," he said, jerking his thumb at the Asian guy. He pointed to the others one by one. "And that's Rush, Kamikaze, and Silk."

"I'm Frank Hardy and this is my brother, Joe."

"Been jumping long?" Squirrel asked.

"Not really," Frank said, "but we did help put out some fires in Montana a while ago."

"We've been hearing a lot about BASE jumping lately," Joe said. He thought he'd introduce the subject casually and watch for a reaction. "Thought we'd get into shape, then try stepping off a building or two."

The group quieted down. Frank and Joe exchanged a quick glance.

Squirrel scratched his three-day-old beard. "No, you guys don't want to get into that. You could get hurt."

"Didn't you hear about that guy who tried to jump off the Metrocorp Building last night?" Rush said.

"No," Joe said. "What about him?"

"Splat." Silk slapped the table with his palm.

"He went in?" Frank asked.

"All the way," Kamikaze said. "His chute got twisted, he hit the building, and boom. D.O.A."

"It was all over the morning news," Squirrel said.

"Okay, so maybe we'll stick to skydiving for now," Frank said.

"We'd better order lunch if we're ever going to get back up in the air," Shima said. "Maybe we'll see you over at the Wild Blue Yonder." He and the others all buried their noses in their menus.

"Probably," Frank said. He and Joe paid for their lunch, stepped outside, and headed straight across the airfield to the Wild Blue Yonder offices. The brothers were about to enter the blue building when, out of the corner of his eye, Joe noticed a man in a maroon windbreaker at the other end of the building. Although he looked to be in his mid-forties, his hair was snow white. He jiggled the handle of a door marked Authorized Personnel Only, opened it a crack, looked left and right, then slipped inside.

Joe motioned to Frank and the two of them strolled over to the door. Frank tried the handle firmly but quietly. It was locked. Joe got out his lock-picking set and went to work. Within seconds he had the door open and the brothers stepped into a cavernous room. It was filled with racks that were neatly stacked with containers, harnesses, helmets, and other jump gear.

Joe caught a glimpse of movement behind one of the racks. He silently pointed, and he and Frank tiptoed in that direction. They approached the rack slowly from either side and peered around it, but there was no one there.

Something metal clanged to the floor on the other side of the room just then, making Joe whirl around in surprise. Next thing Joe knew, the lights went out. He put his hands in front of him and took a step toward where he thought the exit was.

"Frank," he said. "You okay?"

Before he got a reply Joe felt a cloth billow over his head and then engulf him, muffling his brother's outcry and trapping them in total darkness.

Chapter
4

"GRAB ONTO MY SHOULDER, Joe. I think the exit's this way," Frank said, leading them back toward where he thought the door was.

"Frank, we're stuck under a parachute," Joe said.

"No kidding," Frank said, reaching out blindly in front of him. No matter how far they reached in any direction, all they could feel was more cloth.

Joe heard a crash seconds before Frank yelled, "Ow!"

"You okay?" Joe said.

"Yeah, I just bumped my shin." Frank groped along the wall until he felt the door handle. He twisted it, pushed open the door, and the room turned a brilliant yellow.

THE HARDY BOYS CASEFILES

"It's a yellow parachute," Joe said.

"I can see that," Frank said.

Joe tripped over the doorsill, bumped into Frank, and the two of them tumbled onto the ground outside. They fought their way out from under the parachute to the sound of laughter from a small crowd that had gathered around.

"You have an unusual way of testing our equipment," said a tall man in a leather flight jacket and aviator shades. Behind him were Squirrel McCracken and the others they'd met at the Drop Inn, along with a powerfully built man they hadn't seen before.

"Mind if I ask what you were doing in there?" the tall man said.

"Sorry," Frank said. "I guess we got lost. We were looking for the Wild Blue Yonder."

"Right building, wrong door," the man in the flight jacket said. He pointed to the other end of the building. "This door's supposed to be locked. The entrance is over there." He put out his hand. "Anyway, I'm Tomcat Kritzer."

"Joe Hardy," Joe said, shaking his hand. "And this is my brother, Frank."

Kritzer indicated the powerfully built man. "This is Wayne Darcy, my jump supervisor."

"Hi, fellows," Darcy said, shaking their hands. "Are you here to take a class?"

"Well, we're already certified," Joe said.

"That's great," Kritzer said. "But we insist that everyone who jumps with us take a class before-

38

hand. Too many people get their certificates without having any idea of what they're doing."

Frank could see Joe was about to argue the point, so he stepped in. "We'd be glad to take the class." He was thinking it would be a good opportunity to nose around some more.

"Good," Kritzer said.

Darcy, Squirrel, and his friends started off toward a Twin Otter that was idling on the tarmac. "We're going up," Squirrel shouted over his shoulder. "Catch you later."

"Come on." Kritzer waved for Frank and Joe to follow him. "I'll give you the grand tour."

Frank and Joe followed a few steps behind Kritzer. Making sure the man couldn't hear, Frank whispered to Joe, "I wonder where the white-haired guy went."

"You mean the one we followed into the blue building?"

Frank nodded, and Joe said under his breath, "Good question. Keep your eyes open."

Kritzer led them to a hangar that housed several planes in a variety of sizes, all of them new. Two technicians in bright orange overalls were making repairs to the rudder of a twin-engine Cessna.

Frank was impressed. "Looks as though you run a tight ship."

"We follow all the correct procedures," Kritzer said. "And maintenance is a high priority."

Kritzer gave them a quick tour of the facility,

then glanced at his watch. "It's about time for class." The Hardys followed him to a room with windows that featured a panoramic view of the runway. Like everything else it was clean, well lit, and new.

A dozen students were already seated, almost half of them women. Frank and Joe took their seats. Kritzer asked each of the students to explain what they did for a living and why they wanted to jump. Among them was a stockbroker, a secretary, two college students, a female plumber, an artist, and several people in sales. As they went around the room, most of them said they had always dreamed of skydiving or had a friend dare them to give it a try. A few, like the Hardys, had already done some jumping.

When it was Joe's turn, he said, "Hi, everybody. My brother and I are students at Bayport High. We were looking for something to do over the Christmas vacation and we haven't jumped in a while."

"The last time we did any jumping was for the Forest Service in Montana," Frank added. At the time, the Hardys had been much more concerned about the danger of landing in a firestorm than hitting the middle of a drop zone.

"Good," Kritzer said. "I'm glad to hear a few of you have had some jump experience, but I'm going to go over the basics for everyone even if you've heard them a thousand times. We stress safety above all else, because we want you to stay

alive. Dead skydivers make lousy customers."
With that he launched into a lecture on every
aspect of skydiving, drawing diagrams and writing
rapidly on a board with colored markers.

Forty-five minutes later Kritzer turned to the
class and said, "Are there any questions?"

Frank waited for two other students to ask
their questions, then he raised his hand. "We
were wondering about BASE jumping. Can you
help us work on techniques so we can try it out?"

Kritzer's smile faded, replaced by an angry
glare. "There are some people who think jumping off a building, an antenna, a bridge, or a cliff
is a sport. A lot of them don't have the proper
equipment or training to pull it off." He began
pacing up and down in front of the class. "If
something goes wrong, there is much less time to
react, since the ground is usually closer. The
slightest breeze can throw you way off course,
and in the worst cases, right into the object you
jumped off. If your chute doesn't deploy, you're
history. It's incredibly dangerous. There's only
one way to approach BASE jumping: *Don't do
it.*" With his fists on his hips, Kritzer stood directly in front of Frank and demanded, "Are we
clear on that?"

Frank imagined what it must have been like to
have this man as a superior officer in the navy.
"Yes, sir," he said.

The smile returned to Kritzer's tanned face.

"Don't get me wrong—I want you all to have fun. But I want to see you do it safely. Now let's take a break. See you back here in ten minutes. We've got a dynamite videotape of some former pupils in action, so don't be late." With that he strode out of the room.

The Hardys followed the other students outside. Joe spotted a vending machine nearby and treated his brother to a soda. They watched the Wild Blue Yonder's Twin Otter being refueled on the tarmac.

The bus they had ridden from the jump zone earlier pulled up next to the hangar. Squirrel McCracken hopped out carrying what looked like a snowboard. He was followed by the rest of his friends, including Dave Shima, who cradled a helmet with a video camera mounted on top. The group was whooping and hollering.

"I hope you got some good shots this time, Shima," McCracken said. "Because I was really hot up there."

"You can watch yourself on the playback," Shima said.

McCracken turned to the others. "Was I hot or was I hot?"

"Scorching," Rush said. He put a finger on McCracken's shoulder and quickly pulled it back, shaking it as if he'd been burned.

McCracken waved to Frank and Joe. "Hey, guys. We're going up again. Want to come?"

"Try and stop us," Joe shouted back.

42

"Get yourselves some gear," McCracken said. "We'll see you on the Otter in fifteen."

With the help of Dave Shima, Frank and Joe selected jumpsuits, put on harnesses and helmets, and repacked chutes and reserves.

The Twin Otter's door had been removed and its interior stripped of all but the essentials. The jumpers sat on benches that ran along either side of the fuselage. Joe and Frank sat across from Squirrel, who held his sky surfboard across his lap, and Shima, who looked like a coal miner in his camera helmet. The plane taxied to the end of the runway and took off.

When they reached ten thousand feet, still climbing to jumping altitude, Joe glanced down and noticed Squirrel was wearing nothing but sandals on his feet. He shouted over the drone of the plane, "Hey, Squirrel. You forgot your boots."

"No, I didn't." Squirrel wiggled his toes. "I love to feel the wind whistle between my toes."

"Doesn't it hurt when you land?" Frank asked.

"Not if you do it right," Squirrel said.

At thirteen thousand feet Wayne Darcy, the jumper supervisor, looked out the open hatchway, then went up to the cockpit to talk with the pilot. A moment later he returned and addressed the jumpers. "Sorry, folks. Jump's canceled."

The divers groaned. Squirrel sprang to his feet and got in Darcy's face. "What do you mean, canceled?"

"Cloud cover's too thick now. You know the rules."

Squirrel looked out the hatchway. "There are only a couple of clouds over the drop zone. That's nothing."

"C'mon, Darcy, lighten up," Shima said.

"You stay out of this," Darcy snapped. "I'm the supervisor, and if I say we abort the jump, we abort."

Frank and Joe turned and looked out the window. They could make out only patches of the ground through the increasing clouds.

"Visibility's pretty bad out there," Frank said to his brother.

Darcy shouted at McCracken, "There will be no more jumping today. Not in this weather. Understood?" Their faces were now inches apart.

"Perfectly," McCracken said, his face flushed with anger. He started back to his seat, then abruptly turned and darted toward the hatchway. Darcy lunged for McCracken but was too late. McCracken was already out the hatch and in the air.

Before Darcy could recover, Shima and Silk dashed behind him out the hatch. Darcy watched the airborne McCracken roll over on his back and salute as he, Silk, and Shima fell, big grins on their faces.

Everyone else rushed to the hatchway to see the trio quickly disappearing. Then Joe thought he saw a shape, something large and dark, far below in between the clouds.

"Look!" he shouted. Through a break in the clouds he and the others could clearly make out the logo of a popular tire company. "It's a blimp."

McCracken, Silk, and Shima were on a deadly collision course with the huge airship.

Chapter

5

JOE GRABBED A PAIR of high-powered binoculars from the cockpit and scanned the area where McCracken, Silk, and Shima had jumped. He spotted them quickly, free-falling straight toward the airship. "They're going to crash right into it!" he exclaimed.

Just then McCracken's chute popped open, followed immediately by Shima's and then Silk's. They pulled some quick maneuvers and managed to sail past the ungainly airship, missing it by only a few feet.

"They made it," Joe said. Everyone in the plane cheered except Darcy.

"Everybody sit down," Darcy shouted, his eyes flashing anger. "Those fools—all they are is lucky."

*   *   *

When McCracken, Silk, and Shima rolled up to the Wild Blue Yonder in the drop zone bus, Wayne Darcy was waiting for them along with Frank, Joe, and the other jumpers.

"Did you see the look on that blimp pilot's face when he saw us floating past?" McCracken said to Shima. "I couldn't figure out who was more shocked—you or him."

Darcy jabbed a finger at McCracken's chest. "I can't believe you'd pull such a stupid stunt." He looked at Shima and Silk. "What were you idiots thinking?"

McCracken shrugged. "So there was some cloud cover. No big deal."

"Nobody got hurt," Silk said.

"I ought to hurt you now," Darcy said. "You directly disobeyed my order." He was about four inches from McCracken's face. "Don't ever do that again!"

"I—we won't," McCracken said. "You have my word."

"I'm going to speak to Kritzer about this. He ought to ground the three of you for pulling such a stunt. If it was up to me, I'd throw you out of here for good."

McCracken stared defiantly at Darcy and said, "But it's not up to you, is it, Wayne?"

"Watch yourself, McCracken," Darcy said. "You wouldn't want me for an enemy." Then he turned and marched off.

McCracken stood smugly cradling his board in

47

folded arms. "Darcy knows Tomcat needs us for the skysurfing competition tomorrow. Those guys from South Carolina are tough. The Wild Blue Yonder team wouldn't stand a chance without its stars—us."

"I think you might have gone too far this time, Squirrel," Shima said.

McCracken waved Shima off. "No way. After we've whipped those boys from South Carolina, Darcy and Tomcat will be as happy as pigs in slop. They'll forget all about it."

"Tomcat might," Silk said, "but Darcy won't."

"Darcy's all mouth," McCracken scoffed. "Let's head over to the Drop Inn. We should go over our moves for the competition."

The Hardys followed the others toward the diner. Suddenly Joe stopped cold in his tracks and stared at the parking lot.

"What is it?" Frank asked.

"That's it. It's got to be," Joe said. "The yellow van."

"There's only one way to find out," Frank said. They veered off until they got a full view of the van's rear license plate: AW CHUTE.

"That proves that whoever jumped off that building with Kurt Waller is here today," Joe said.

Frank shook his head. "No. All it proves is that a van that was near the Metrocorp Building last night is at Ridgeway Airport today. We need a lot more than this to tie things together."

"I guess you're right," Joe said. "But let's check it out anyway."

Frank surveyed the lot to make sure they weren't being watched while Joe moved in for a closer look. He tried the driver's door but found it locked. He peered in the window looking for evidence of the van's ownership. All he could see were coffee cups and fast-food containers on the floor, along with an old skydiving magazine addressed to a T. Randall.

"I hope this T. Randall hasn't flown out of town on a long trip," Joe said.

"So do I," Frank replied. "The van might have even been abandoned or stolen. I say we grab something to eat and keep an eye on it from the Drop Inn."

They ate dinner with McCracken and company while Shima played back the videotape of their narrow miss with the blimp on a minicam. They took turns watching it in the tiny viewer screen.

One minute McCracken's and Silk's chutes opened, and the next minute the frame filled with blimp. Then there was a split-second shot of the blimp crew's startled expressions as they watched the skydivers sail past. All the while, Frank kept his eyes glued to the yellow van.

"Well, I'm out of here," Silk said, having finished his second piece of apple pie. "Anyone who wants a lift better hustle."

McCracken, Shima, Rush, and Kamikaze picked

up their gear and headed for the door behind Silk.

Shima turned to the Hardys. "You guys gonna come by tomorrow to watch the competition?"

"It should be awesome," McCracken said.

"We wouldn't miss it," Joe said. He waited until the others had left, then said to Frank, "I hope the owner of that van shows up soon. I'm not up for an all-night stakeout."

"Neither am I," Frank said. "And you just got your wish." He and Joe watched Silk unlock the yellow van and get into the driver's seat while McCracken and Shima climbed in on the other side. Kamikaze and Rush went to another part of the lot.

The Hardys paid their check in a hurry, went out, and hopped into their van. Joe fired up the engine. "I wonder if Silk is T. Randall."

"Just follow them and maybe we'll find out," Frank said.

The yellow van pulled out of the lot onto the highway, the Hardys tailing at a discreet distance. After several miles, it turned into a quiet residential neighborhood. When the van rolled into the driveway of a neatly kept house, Joe drove straight past while Frank jotted down the address in his note pad.

Joe pulled around the next corner and stopped. They watched from behind a tall hedge as McCracken jumped out of the passenger side and disappeared into the house. Then the van headed toward the center of Ridgeway, where it stopped across the street from the train station. Shima got out and went in a doorway next to a dingy, neon-lit club called the Frolic Room. A moment later they saw a light come on in an upstairs window.

"Shima's place looks pretty run-down," Frank said.

"Skydiving's not a cheap sport," Joe said. "He must be saving money on rent."

Next they tailed the yellow van to a large apartment complex a few blocks from Shima's. They followed Silk around back to a garage. He punched some numbers into a keypad, the gate rolled open, and the yellow van disappeared inside.

"Well," Frank said, entering the address in his notebook, "we know where some of the jumpers live, but not much else. Let's head home."

When the brothers got home it was only a little after nine o'clock. They found their father hard at work in front of the computer in his office. "Hi, guys," he said wearily, taking off his reading glasses and rubbing the bridge of his nose.

"How's Phil's new drive working out?" Frank asked.

"Great. But it's going to take me a while to get up to speed. Sergeant Williams called with some information for you." He began to read from a pink memo sheet on his desk. "That yellow van is registered to—"

"Let me guess," Joe interrupted, "a T. Randall of Ridgeway."

Fenton smiled. "You beat me to the punch. His first name's Timothy."

"And his nickname's Silk," Frank added. "We found the van parked out at Ridgeway Municipal Airport," he explained.

"Anything else?" Fenton asked.

"Kurt Waller was jumping without his parents' permission," Joe said.

"He was skydiving at Ridgeway," Frank added. "They've got two rival schools over there. We know he took lessons from at least one of them, but nobody's talking about him or about any BASE jumping."

"We need more on these schools," Joe said. "Maybe we should start with the Federal Aviation Administration."

"I have a friend over there, Bob Edgewater," Fenton said. "We worked together on that skyjacking case I had about ten years ago." He switched to the address book program in his computer. "Hope he hasn't moved. I used to have his home number." Within seconds Bob Edgewater's entry appeared on the screen. Fenton selected Autodial from a menu and his modem dialed the phone. After one ring, a man's voice came on the speaker phone: "Hello."

"Bob Edgewater?" Fenton said.

"Speaking. Who's this?"

"Fenton Hardy. Remember me?"

"Of course." Edgewater sounded sincerely glad to hear from Fenton. "You nailed that skyjacker just about single-handedly. What brings you out of the woodwork?"

"My sons are working on a case for me, and they need some information about a couple of skydiving schools. I thought you'd be able to help."

"I'll do what I can."

Frank spoke into the speakerphone. "Hi, Mr. Edgewater. This is Frank Hardy."

"And I'm Joe," his brother said.

"Hello, Frank, Joe. How can I help you?"

"What can you tell us about a couple of schools called the Johnson Jump Academy and the Wild Blue Yonder?" Frank said.

"They're located at Ridgeway Municipal," Joe added.

There was a long pause at the other end of the line. "Are you still there?" Fenton asked.

Finally, Bob Edgewater replied. "Yeah. I'm not familiar with them myself, but I'll beat the bushes and we'll see what flies out."

"Thanks, Mr. Edgewater," Frank said. "We really appreciate it."

"Give me a day or two. And if you haven't heard from me, call." He gave them his office number, said goodbye to Fenton, and hung up.

"He's one of the good guys," Fenton said. "If anyone can help you out, it's Bob."

The next morning Joe and Frank awoke to an unseasonably warm day, with the temperature in the fifties and not a cloud in the sky.

"Should be perfect weather for the competition," Joe said as he and Frank stepped out of their van at the Ridgeway Airport. Next to the runway sat an immaculate purple DC3 they'd never seen before. The Sky's the Limit, Lakeville, South Carolina was printed in white on the fuselage. Frank and Joe joined a crowd that had gathered inside the Wild Blue Yonder hangar. The planes had all been moved out onto the tarmac, and large-screen video monitors now hung from the ceiling of the hangar. The image of a skydiver doing flips and spins filled the screens.

"I guess we're going to have to watch the competition on TV," Joe said to Frank.

"I guess so," Frank replied, "but the action still looks pretty hot to me."

Tomcat Kritzer saw the Hardys from the far side of the hangar and came over. "I'm glad you two could make it. Our team's going up first, then we'll alternate for the rest of the day with the Carolina team. It'll be nonstop action."

"Sounds exciting," Frank said. "We only wish we could see it from closer up."

"I might be able to arrange that," Kritzer offered.

"That'd be great," Joe said.

"Two of the contestants had to drop out at the last minute," Kritzer said. "We can't let you compete, but since you do have jump experience, I don't see why you can't suit up and watch from the air."

"Let's do it," Frank said.

Frank and Joe were given jumpsuits, helmets, a pair of parasails to repack, and harnesses to slip into. Within minutes they found themselves in a Twin Otter with Squirrel McCracken, Dave Shima, and the rest of the Ridgeway team on their way toward the drop zone. Squirrel and another jumper, who was named Eddie, had sky-surfing boards, while Shima and several others wore helmets with cameras attached to them. Frank counted two dozen jumpers in all.

Frank and Joe watched Squirrel, who was sitting directly across from them in the open cabin, close his eyes and go into what looked like a trance. He held his hand out in front of him and started swooping and swerving it as if it were a plane.

Frank leaned over to Silk and said, "Do you think Squirrel's okay?"

"He's just rehearsing his routine. Every move is totally planned so Dave can follow him with the camera. The video is all the judges get to see, so good camera work and coordination are critical."

As they approached the drop zone, Wayne Darcy took his position by the door, and the jumpers lined up. Darcy tapped each on the shoulder, sending them on their way out into the sky. Joe was impressed to see him treat Squirrel and his friends no differently from anyone else when it was their turn to jump, despite the ugly scene the day before.

Frank and Joe were the last out of the plane. The sight that greeted them as they dived toward the earth was awesome. Two groups of jumpers were linking up in complicated formations, unlinking, and then linking up again.

Squirrel McCracken was surfing the sky as if he were shredding waves. Dave Shima covered the action with his camera helmet from a few yards away. The Hardys noticed Dave's jumpsuit had been specially designed with fabric "wings" between his arms and body that allowed him to adjust his speed to match McCracken's.

Frank watched as Squirrel went into a fast spin one way, then abruptly stopped and went the other way. Then he executed a series of 360-degree flips. Every time he aimed the board toward the ground, he suddenly sped up as if he were dropping down the face of a thirty-footer off the north shore of Oahu.

Meanwhile, Joe kept his eye on Eddie, the other jumper with a board. His moves were just as impressive. "Radical," Joe said, his words yanked away by the wind.

Frank signaled to Joe and pointed off in the

distance. The air was so clear they could see the skyline of downtown Bayport more than thirty miles away. Then it happened. Joe saw the sky-surfer Eddie and his camera-flyer collide head-on. They hit hard and began to drop like rag dolls toward the ground.

Chapter

6

JOE LOOKED AROUND to see if any of the others had seen the collision, but it didn't look as if they had. He signaled to Frank again and pointed down at what were quickly becoming two specks against the landscape.

Joe followed Natalie's example from the day before, diving headfirst toward the falling jumpers. Frank immediately followed his lead. With arms at their sides, the Hardys were like two peregrine falcons closing in on their prey.

Joe got to them first. He had to back off a couple of times to avoid a flailing arm or leg. He saw that both jumpers were unconscious. Timing his approach, Joe grabbed Eddie in a half nelson

58

and attached his harness to the diver's rig while Frank grabbed the camera-flyer.

Frank quickly checked the altimeter attached to his harness. They were less than two thousand feet from the ground, about twenty seconds from impact. He'd never popped his chute this low before. He knew it was possible to deploy at well under one thousand feet, but he also knew the lower he did, the harder he'd land and the smaller his margin for error.

Frank and Joe pulled their rip cords and drifted toward the ground. Eddie blinked his eyes open before impact, giving him time to prepare to land with Joe. The camera-flyer, however, was still unconscious, landing with Frank a few yards away from Joe with a heavy thud. They were in a field about a quarter mile from the drop zone.

"Frank, you okay?" Joe yelled, rushing up to his brother.

Frank nodded his head. "Yeah." He was pinned by the unmoving camera-flyer, who Joe could see was a woman. "Help me out of here, will you?"

Joe unhooked Frank's harness and carefully lifted the camera-flyer just enough for Frank to scramble out. Joe gently tapped the unconscious jumper's cheek. She didn't respond.

"We've got to get help fast," Joe said.

"It's already on the way," Frank said. They heard the wail of a siren in the distance, then saw an ambulance bouncing over the field toward them. Joe waved his arms over his head.

The paramedics brought the camera-flyer around with smelling salts, then examined her and the skysurfer.

"They both definitely have concussions," one of the paramedics said. "The guy may have a broken collarbone, but we won't know for sure till we see X-rays."

As the paramedics were loading the victims into the ambulance, Squirrel and the other jumpers marched up and shook hands with Frank and Joe. "Nice save, guys," Squirrel said.

"Couldn't have done better myself," Silk said.

"Good work," Shima added.

"We just happened to be at the right place at the right time," Frank said.

"I wish there was some way we could get you into the competition," Squirrel said. "But you have to be with one of the schools and register way in advance."

"Thanks," Frank said, "but I think that was enough excitement for one day."

"Speak for yourself," Joe said. "I'd like to get in a few more jumps, if it's all right with Tomcat."

Shima took off his helmet and tucked it under his arm. "Don't worry, when Kritzer finds out about this, I'm sure he'll let you do anything you like."

When they got back to the airport, Kritzer was

the first to rush over and congratulate the Hardys on their dramatic rescue. "All your jumps are on the house through the end of Christmas vacation," he said.

"Thanks, Tomcat," Joe said.

"You're very generous," Frank said.

"You saved my school an awful lot of grief, not to mention a couple of lives," Kritzer said.

Joe spent the rest of the day taking as many jumps as he could, while Frank watched the competition from the hangar. That way they figured they had both the sky and the ground covered.

Near the end of the day, the Sky's the Limit was ahead of the Wild Blue Yonder on points, but Squirrel performed a near-perfect routine on his last jump. He executed every single maneuver without a hitch, and Shima's video was right on the money. It was enough to put the home team over the top. When the competition was over, Frank and Joe joined the other jumpers for a victory celebration at the Drop Inn.

"It's on me," Kritzer proclaimed to raucous cheering, and they were all served sodas and pizzas. Kritzer held his glass up high and said, "I'd like to make a toast. To everyone who had anything to do with today's performance, I salute you." They all raised their glasses and drank, then cheered some more. Kritzer circled the room, shaking hands with jumpers and crew members. He finished his drink and said,

"There's still some cleaning up to do, so I'll see you all later. Congratulations again." He waved and left for the hangar.

"Was that competition extreme, or what?" Squirrel shouted.

"Gnarly, dudes!" someone called out, and everyone roared in agreement.

In the middle of the festivities, Joe spotted a television set sitting on a shelf behind the lunch counter. The picture was on without the sound. A shot of a jumper drifting to earth under a parasail was followed by a close-up of Janice Gainey, the reporter for *The Real Deal* tabloid show. Joe remembered seeing her in front of the Wallers' house the day before. Below her face was the station's logo and the word *Live!* Someone turned up the sound and the room quickly fell silent.

"Police here in Bellington, New Jersey, report that several people jumped from the WZZM tower last night," Gainey said. The camera zoomed out to show a tall radio antenna behind her. The picture cut to an older man in a security uniform. "Around midnight," he said, "my partner and I saw several parachuters on one of the security monitors. We ran outside in time to see the last two land."

"Here is the actual videotape these security personnel saw," Janice Gainey said, "taken by the facility's closed-circuit camera."

The image cut to a grainy black-and-white shot of a jumper landing at night under floodlights.

"How do you suppose these people got into your facility and climbed the tower in the first place?" Gainey asked.

The guard looked uncomfortable. "We're looking into it and taking measures to beef up security so this kind of thing doesn't happen again."

"Yeah, right!" shouted someone at the lunch counter, prompting laughter.

The camera zoomed in on Gainey. "This is the second instance of skydivers jumping from a structure in the New York area in the past two days. If you'll recall, seventeen-year-old Kurt Waller died jumping from the Metrocorp Building in Manhattan on Friday night.

"Is this the work of the same people, or the start of a horrifying new trend?" Gainey continued. "Authorities either don't know or won't say. So you'll have to judge for yourselves. Back to you in the studio, Marcus." A news anchor came on the screen and someone turned down the sound.

Silk put his hand to his mouth, trembling as if afraid, and shouted, "Oh, how horrifying!" This brought more laughter from the Wild Blue Yonder crowd.

"What do you think about this latest BASE jump?" Frank asked Joe on their way home a half hour later. "Is it the same guys?"

"That security tape was so blurry I couldn't tell. What do you think?"

Frank pulled into the Hardys' driveway. "I saw Squirrel and Silk give each other funny looks while they watched the news coverage. That could mean they were the jumpers, or maybe they're just happy to see someone pull off a stunt like that."

They got out of the van and headed for the house. Joe stopped at the kitchen door. "How about three accidents in three days?" he said.

"It's a lot," Frank said. "Even for a dangerous sport like skydiving."

"It could be sabotage," Joe said.

"It *could,*" Frank said. "That collision with Eddie and the camerawoman this afternoon sure looked like an accident. And we couldn't find anything wrong with my chute that didn't open. The one I'm still not so sure about is Kurt Waller."

Joe thought for a moment. "It would help if we could establish a solid connection between Kurt and the guys at Wild Blue Yonder. So far it's pretty iffy."

"We've also got to ask what possible motive anyone could have for causing these accidents," Frank said.

They went into the kitchen, which was filled with the delicious smell of dinner cooking. Fenton, wearing an apron, had the oven door open and was basting a lamb roast, while their mother tossed a salad. "Hi, guys," she said. "Just in time for dinner."

"Must be our lucky day," Joe said.

"We'll wash up and be right down," Frank said.

On their way upstairs they passed Aunt Gertrude. "Good evening, Frank, Joe," she said. "Someone named Rob Endwatcher called asking for the two of you."

"Was it Bob Edgewater by any chance?" Frank asked.

"Isn't that what I said? Anyway, I wrote down his number." She fished a note out of her cardigan pocket and handed it to Frank. "He asked you to call immediately."

Frank made the call right away. The FAA investigator picked up on the first ring. "Edgewater," he said.

"It's Frank Hardy, Mr. Edgewater."

"Thanks for getting back to me, Frank. Can you and your brother meet me at my office at Kennedy International Airport in an hour?"

"Sure," Frank said. "What's this all about?"

"I'll fill you in when you get here." Edgewater gave Frank directions to FAA headquarters and hung up.

"What's he got?" Joe said.

"He just said to be at his office in an hour."

Frank and Joe watched their parents setting platters of food on the dining table. "That gives us fifteen minutes to eat dinner," Joe said. "Plenty of time."

The brothers plowed through their meal, while Fenton recalled details on the case he'd worked on with Bob Edgewater. Thirteen minutes later, Frank and Joe excused themselves from the table, ran out to the van, and headed for JFK International. They made good time on the expressway until traffic slowed to a crawl less than a mile from the terminal.

"At this rate," Frank said, "we'll be lucky to get to Edgewater's office before Valentine's Day. We'd be better off walking."

"Holiday traffic," Joe said from behind the wheel. "Everybody goes on vacation at the same time. Keep your eyes out for a parking space."

They listened to Christmas carols on the radio as the van crept along, passing several parking structures before finding one without a Lot Full sign. After parking the van on the roof, they walked to the nearest terminal. "Where did Edgewater say his office was?" Joe said.

"From here I'm not sure. Let's ask."

The brothers headed for an information kiosk. While Joe asked an attendant for directions to the FAA offices, Frank scanned the throngs of travelers milling about. In the middle of the crowd he spotted a tall man who looked familiar. "The guy in the suit who just walked by—do we know him?" he asked Joe.

Joe thanked the attendant and turned to Frank. "I didn't see anyone."

Frank racked his brain trying to place the man's face. Then it came to him. "It's that white-haired guy who was snooping around the Wild Blue Yonder."

"You mean the one who dropped the parachute on us?"

"That's the one. Let's go after him," Frank said, picking up his pace. "If we split up, just meet me at Edgewater's office," Frank shouted back over his shoulder.

Frank moved quickly through the terminal, peering over heads to keep track of the man in the suit. There were so many faces that the task seemed impossible. He was about to give up when he spotted the man leaving the terminal. Frank fought his way through a group of people carrying ski gear, then ran straight into another group in Hawaiian shirts and shorts. When he finally made his way outside, the man was nowhere in sight.

Frank heard Joe behind him. "Frank! He went that way."

Frank saw his brother caught in the middle of the Hawaiian delegation, pointing down the sidewalk to his left. Frank broke into a jog, dodging knots of people waiting at curbside. He scanned the area, finally catching a glimpse of his target walking quickly away from the terminals and down a stairway to the lower level.

Frank hustled down the stairs. Looking quickly around, he saw the man approach an office building and go through a door marked Authorized Personnel Only. Frank ran to the door. It opened onto a stairwell that led up to another door that was just closing. He bounded up the stairs, opened the second door, and found himself in a long corridor. The man turned a corner at the other end. Frank ran after him and rounded the corner in time to see yet another door close before he could get to it. The door was labeled 2078-G. He turned around to see his brother coming up fast.

"He's on the other side of this door," Frank said, lowering his voice.

Joe made a move to reach around his brother and grab the handle.

"Hold it," Frank said. "He could be armed."

"Hey, there are two of us," Joe said. "We can handle him."

"Just be ready for anything," Frank said. "I'll go first. Stand back."

Joe took a step back while Frank turned the handle. He cracked the door open an inch and saw that the room was pitch-black. Swiftly, Frank opened the door wide and strode into the darkness.

The next thing Joe knew, the door was slammed in his face and there was a thud on the other side of it—a thud that he was afraid could mean only one thing: Frank was in trouble.

"Hey! Hey! What are you doing in there? Open up," Joe shouted. He banged on the door with his fists, tried the handle, and banged some more. There was another thud and then silence, and Joe feared the worst. He shouted and threw all his weight into the door, but it wouldn't budge. "Frank? Frank?" he cried out.

But he got no answer.

Chapter

7

JOE WAS GETTING DESPERATE. His brother wasn't answering him, and the door wouldn't give. He listened for a moment and thought he heard voices. Deciding there was only one thing to do, he backed up about ten steps so he could take a running start toward the door. Hoping his prowess on the football field wouldn't fail him, he leaned his shoulder toward the door and started running like a linebacker.

But just when he expected to feel the painful crunch of his shoulder meeting the resistance of the wood, the door swung open. Joe went sailing through and, skidding, came to a crashing halt. The lights were on, and he saw that he'd been stopped by a copy machine.

Stunned, he looked up to see the white-haired man extending a hand. "Joe Hardy, nice to meet you. I'm Bob Edgewater."

Joe's mouth dropped open as he realized the mistake he and his brother had made. He absently stuck out his hand, which Edgewater shook.

"But, Frank," Joe said, looking from one to the other. "What was going on in here? It sounded like you were getting the life pounded out of you."

"Actually, I was the one who got the pounding," Mr. Edgewater said.

"I'm really sorry about that," Frank said. "Really, I—"

"Don't mention it," Edgewater said, brushing off his sleeves. "At least now I know you guys mean business. Fenton would be proud of you," he added.

"We saw you snooping around the Wild Blue Yonder yesterday. I guess we almost blew your cover," Joe said, recovering from the surprise. "Sorry," he added.

"No harm done," Edgewater said. "From what your father told me, you're pretty good at undercover work. There's no way that crowd would accept me, but you've got a shot at it. So let's review the case." Edgewater nodded at the young woman standing by a desk in the corner of the office. "Shirley Bascombe, meet Joe and Frank Hardy. Shirley's my assistant," he explained.

"She's working her way up to investigator. Right, Shirley?"

"Just learning from the master," she said with a smile.

"And she's already learned that a little flattery goes a long way. Shirley, would you please pull the Ridgeway Municipal file?"

"Coming up." She went through a cabinet drawer, found the file, and handed it to her boss.

"We've got plenty of background on Johnson and Kritzer," Edgewater said, reading from a computer printout. "Johnson was a paratrooper in Korea from fifty-two to fifty-four, then he got pilot training and flew combat in Vietnam. He was awarded medals for bravery, but he also got busted a few times for pulling crazy stunts. He's had his license lifted more than once. Johnson might be the kind of guy to promote daredevil stuff like BASE jumping, even if he's too old for it himself."

"To tell you the truth, it didn't look like he had enough of a following in Ridgeway to organize a game of tennis," Frank said.

"And we're not talking doubles," Joe added.

"Let's look at Kritzer then." Edgewater pulled out another printout. "He flew Tomcats for the navy, was honorably discharged with an impeccable record. I've got nothing to report on his school. The guy's so clean he practically squeaks."

"He seems to maintain that image," Frank said.

Edgewater frowned. "I've got to wonder about the level of training at Kritzer's school, though. Kurt Waller was taking lessons at the Wild Blue Yonder and look what happened to him."

"We haven't actually found out if he was a student there," Frank said.

"He was," Edgewater said. "I pulled the Wild Blue Yonder roster."

"I still don't think it was Kurt's fault," Frank said. "The way his chute opened, the first thing I'd wonder is if somebody tampered with it."

Edgewater shook his head. "I examined that chute myself, and there was absolutely no evidence of any foul play."

"So you're definitely ruling it an accident?" Joe said.

"No," Edgewater said, "but right now my goal is to find out who's behind this BASE jumping and stop it before someone else gets hurt."

"Is there any link between that radio tower jump and the Metrocorp one?" Joe said.

"Not that I know of, but you two just might be able to help." Edgewater gave the Hardys a serious look. "I have to warn you, though—if your cover gets blown, neither I nor the FAA can admit we've even heard of you."

Joe nodded his head. "We understand."

Edgewater scribbled on a slip of paper and handed it to Frank. "Here's my pager number.

My response time is pretty quick—any time of day. You're welcome to phone in 'anonymous tips' if you've got anything. Whatever you do, be careful."

"We will," Joe said.

After Edgewater wished them luck, Frank and Joe left the office and made their way back to the van. "I sure hope we don't have to meet Bob Edgewater by surprise again," Frank said. "I'm getting tired of wiping the egg off my face."

"Me, too," Joe said.

Frank and Joe spent most of the next day working on their jumping techniques. They sky-surfed for a while, then, at the suggestion of Tomcat Kritzer, attempted to fly some formations. Kritzer said it would be simple, but coming together in midair, locking arms, quickly changing positions, and spinning all turned out to be much harder than it looked.

Late that afternoon the Hardys were on their way to the Drop Inn to refuel when they saw Silk's yellow van pulling into the parking lot. Silk, Squirrel, and Shima got out, followed by Kamikaze and Rush.

"Where have you guys been all day?" Frank said.

Squirrel had a sour look on his face. "Kritzer grounded us. Darcy actually ratted on us for jumping against orders the other day. Can you believe it?"

"What a shame," Frank said, even though he completely agreed with Kritzer's decision.

"Don't worry," Joe said. "I'm sure it'll blow over in a day or two."

Squirrel smiled. "Yeah, well, I'm not waiting around for His Highness to come to his senses."

"What do you mean?" Frank asked.

Squirrel leaned forward and lowered his voice. "We're going to do a little jumping on our own."

Joe looked perplexed. "Who's going to take you up, Spencer Johnson?"

"Are you kidding?" Squirrel said. "We don't need a plane."

"So what are you talking about?" Frank asked.

Squirrel leaned even closer, his voice barely above a whisper. "How would you guys like to try a little BASE jumping?"

"Sure," Joe said, "I've been kind of itching to . . ."

Frank shook his head. "I don't know, Joe. They didn't see us trying to fly formations today. Not a pretty sight."

"Believe me," Silk said, "there isn't any formation flying involved. All you do is step off, open your chute, and land."

"It's the biggest rush you'll ever experience," Squirrel added. "Are you with us?"

Frank and Joe looked at each other. "Count us in," Joe said.

"All right," Silk said, motioning them over to the van. "Take a look at some gear." He slid open the door to reveal neatly stowed racks holding every imaginable kind of skydiving equipment.

Shima pulled out a parachute shell. "This is the kind of chute we use. It's a 'square' with two layers of fabric. It deploys much faster."

If there was any doubt that these were Kurt Waller's companions on his final jump, it was erased when Shima handed them jumpsuits with flying-reptile shoulder patches, just like the one Waller was wearing.

"What's this?" Frank asked.

"Our mascot," Silk said. "We're the Leaping Lizards."

"Let's move out," Squirrel said.

"By the way," Joe said, "did any of you know that guy who bought it jumping off the Metrocorp Building?"

Shima shook his head—almost too quickly. "Nope." He looked around at his friends. "Anybody else know him?" They all shook their heads.

Joe noticed an unnatural silence among them and wondered what it meant.

"Can you guys wait a few minutes?" Frank said. He knew he should contact Bob Edgewater, especially with a BASE jump coming up. "I've got to make a call."

"Have to let Mom know her boys won't be home for dinner?" Kamikaze said. The others laughed.

"I had a date with my girlfriend," Frank said,

sounding slightly annoyed. "If I don't call, I may not have a girlfriend anymore."

Squirrel looked at his watch. "All right, but we're out of here in exactly two minutes."

Frank jogged to a pay phone next to the Drop Inn, dialed Edgewater's office, and left a message with Shirley. "Just let him know we're onto some BASE jumpers," he told her. "We'll be in touch. Gotta run."

Frank hung up the phone and hustled back to the van. He jumped in the sliding door just as Silk shifted into gear and sped out of the lot. Silk drove onto the expressway heading toward New York City. On the way, the Hardys learned their target for the evening was the Chrysler Building.

When the yellow van got to midtown Manhattan, it took about ten minutes to find a parking space. As the jumpers piled out, Squirrel slowly turned his gaze skyward. "There she is."

Frank, Joe, and the others all looked up. The famous needle-topped skyscraper's upper tiers were bathed in floodlights.

"Wait till you get a load of the view from up there," Silk said.

"You scouted it?" Frank said.

"Silk and I went up a few days ago," Shima said.

"Any surprises?" Frank asked.

"It gets a little tricky at the thirty-first floor,

THE HARDY BOYS CASEFILES

where the building flares out," Shima replied, "but otherwise it's a piece of cake."

Although he and his brother had entered plenty of buildings uninvited to gather evidence for cases, Frank had always been uneasy about it. Tackling the seventy-eight-story, 1,046-foot Chrysler Building, once second only to the Empire State Building as the world's tallest, was a feat he'd never dreamed of attempting.

"Everybody has to sign in on the ground floor," Silk said. "We found three companies that stay open almost around the clock, so we're going in by twos, posing as messengers." He handed out slips of paper. "There's an empty office for rent on sixty-one. We meet there."

"Dave and I go first," Squirrel said. "Frank and Joe, you wait ten minutes and go up, then Silk and Kamikaze bring up the rear ten minutes after that."

"What about Rush?" Joe said.

"I'm the designated driver," Rush said.

"We need to make a quick getaway," Shima said. "Otherwise, we spend the night in the slammer."

"So let's get going," Squirrel said.

They stowed their chutes, jumpsuits, and helmets in lightweight duffel bags.

"We'll see you all on sixty-one," Shima said. He and Squirrel slung their duffels over their shoulders and strode off.

Ten minutes later Frank and Joe pushed through

78

the revolving doors into the lobby, where a security guard sat behind a counter. They showed their fake messenger slips and signed in as Mike Tenneson and Nick Oates of Jet Delivery. Then they got in one of the elevators, which shot them up to the sixty-first floor. When they stepped out there was no one in the hallway. Frank saw a silhouette on the other side of a frosted-glass door down the hall and grabbed Joe, telling him to stop. They quickly pressed against the wall until Shima emerged from the glass door.

"In here, guys," he said in a loud whisper.

Frank and Joe joined him and Squirrel in the empty office.

"Take a look at this spot," Squirrel said. He opened a corner window and crawled outside. The others joined him on a balcony that jutted out from the building in the shape of a giant eagle's head. Squirrel spread out his arms and surveyed the city all around them. "Is this cool or what?"

"It's pretty incredible," Joe said. The night sky over Manhattan was crystal clear, with a few wispy clouds and plenty of stars visible. Skyscrapers were lit up all around, and he glimpsed the world-famous Christmas tree at Rockefeller Center, about eight blocks away.

The four of them went back inside to wait for Silk and Kamikaze, who showed just after ten o'clock. Everyone got into their jumpsuits, then put on their chutes and helmets. Squirrel climbed out onto the eagle's head and said, "Remember, wait until you're as close to the ground as you can get before deploying. The wind up here'll toss you around like a paper airplane once your chute's open."

Squirrel stepped to the edge of the eagle's head, shouted "Yahoo!" and, without hesitation, dived toward the street below. The others watched him drop out of sight until his chute billowed open a couple of seconds later. He glided over toward the yellow van. Next Silk took a few deep breaths, psyching himself up. He climbed onto the eagle's head and jumped. Kamikaze followed right behind him.

"You're up," Shima said to Joe, who stepped out on the eagle's head and looked down. He could feel his heart pounding as he looked down at the tiny cars. This is the craziest thing I've ever done for a case, he thought. But there's no turning back now. "Geronimo!" he yelled, and stepped off.

Windows raced by him in a blur. He felt as if they were closing in on him and he would crash into one any second. He pulled his rip cord and felt the parasail jerk open overhead. It took a couple of seconds to figure out which way he was supposed to be headed. The wind tugged him one way, then another, and he pulled hard on the control lines to steady his descent.

Diving out of an airplane into an open field wasn't the same as BASE jumping. He didn't think he had ever been so terrified or exhilarated in his entire life. As he got closer to the ground he became aware of honking horns and people shouting. He angled past the yellow van, where Squirrel and Silk were stowing their chutes, and landed half a block away in the middle of a side street.

Joe quickly gathered his chute and looked up in time to see Frank's canopy open. His brother came dangerously close to crashing into the building across the street. He made a correction, then another, before drifting to a safe landing. Joe helped Frank reel in his chute.

"Well, at least we're in one piece," Frank said.

Joe could hardly contain his excitement. "What a rush, though, huh?" He and Frank ran back to join the others at the van.

From where they stood, Shima was barely visible near the top of the Chrysler Building. He jumped and went into a free fall. Within seconds he was already halfway down and his chute still hadn't opened.

"Oh, man, he's not going to make it," Joe said as he watched Shima hurtling down toward them.

Chapter

8

AFTER SEVERAL SECONDS of stunned silence, the six jumpers finally saw Shima's chute spread open no more than a dozen stories above the ground. It slowed him down, but a sudden gust of wind hurled him back toward the Chrysler Building. He managed to lift his feet and push off the side of the building.

The jumpers on the ground breathed a collective sigh of relief, but Shima was still dropping fast and not in control. He tried to glide out toward the yellow van, but the wind suddenly died and dropped him hard on top of a delivery truck parked a block away.

"Looks bad," Joe said.

"We'll go get him," Frank said to the others. "You guys bring the van around."

Frank and Joe ran to the truck, jumped on its hood, and scrambled up the cab to the roof. Shima sat clutching his stomach and his face was pale.

"What is it?" Joe said.

"Can't . . . breathe . . ." Shima said, just above a whisper.

Frank heard sirens growing louder in the distance. "Does it hurt anywhere else?" he asked desperately. They were running out of time.

Shima shook his head.

"Then let's get out of here," Joe said.

The Hardys grabbed Shima's gear and helped him down off the truck.

The yellow van rolled up and Squirrel asked, "Is he okay?"

"It's too soon to tell," Joe said, piling into the van behind Shima. "Possible bruised or broken ribs, possible internal injuries."

"I knew you could pull it out," Squirrel said to Shima.

Shima began to breathe easier. "I didn't mean to wait so long. My rip cord was jammed. Guess it came loose just in time."

Squirrel helped Shima out of his harness. "We can check your gear when we get back home."

"Let's move," Silk shouted.

Rush maneuvered the van out of its parking space just as two police cars, lights flashing, sped past in the direction of the Chrysler Building.

"That was close," Silk said.

83

"Good timing, everybody," Squirrel said. "Now back to Ridgeway."

Rush guided the van onto the FDR Drive south, which took them safely out of Manhattan via the Brooklyn Bridge. Gradually, the color started to come back to Shima's face. As they got closer to home, he even began to joke about his near accident. Privately, Frank and Joe both wondered the same thing: was it an accident at all—or a case of serial sabotage?

About an hour later, Silk's van pulled up next to the Hardys' parking spot back at Ridgeway Airport, and the brothers hopped out the side door.

"Thanks a lot, guys," Joe said. "That was a real thrill."

Squirrel leaned out the passenger-side window. "Glad to have you with us. You did great."

"When can we do it again?" Frank asked.

"Real soon," Squirrel replied with a wink.

The yellow van pulled away, leaving the Hardys standing next to their black one in the brightly lit parking lot. As he dug in his pocket for his keys, Joe saw Natalie walking toward them.

"I see you've made some new friends," she said as soon as she was close enough to be heard.

"What are you talking about?" Joe asked.

"I saw McCracken and that bunch drop you off."

"They've been giving us some pointers on how to improve our jumping," Joe said. "That's all."

"I'll bet," Natalie said with a scowl.

"Why do you care so much about who we hang around with?" Frank asked.

"I don't," she said, her voice rising. "Forget it."

"Something's definitely bothering you," Joe said. "We're all ears."

Natalie's lower lip began to quiver. She tried to fight back the tears but couldn't. Frank handed her a tissue from their van. She took it and started tremulously, "Kurt was hanging around with them for a while before he . . . he . . ." She couldn't bring herself to finish.

"Kurt Waller?" Frank asked. "How well did you know him? Were you—"

Natalie shook her head. "It wasn't romantic, if that's what you're asking. Kurt was just a nice kid, and we became good friends. He even introduced me to his parents."

"We met his father," Joe said. "So you think Kurt was with Squirrel and his friends the night he died?"

"Who else?" Natalie sniffed. "That Squirrel's crazy, and Silk Randall's probably worse."

"Do you think any of them might sabotage a jump?" Frank said.

Natalie gave Frank a suspicious look. "What's with all the questions? You're starting to sound like cops."

85

Frank glanced at his brother, as if to ask, Should we tell her the truth? Joe nodded back.

"Our father's a private investigator and sometimes we get involved in cases," Frank explained.

"You're detectives?" Natalie furrowed her brow. "Aren't you kind of young for that?"

"Yeah, but our dad's a good teacher," Joe said.

"Joe and I happened to witness what happened the night Kurt died," Frank said. "We're helping his parents, trying to figure out the truth."

"I want to help, too," Natalie said, wiping away the last of her tears.

"Good," Frank said. "But it could get dangerous. And you might not like what we dig up."

"I don't care. I'd like to know why my friend died."

Joe tried to ask his question delicately, knowing Natalie would be sensitive to what he was suggesting. "Is it possible Spencer Johnson tampered with Kurt's chute to make Kritzer's operation look bad?"

"Oh, please," Natalie shot back. "Spencer would never do something like that."

"We found out from the FAA that Spencer pulled some pretty wild stunts when he was in the service," Frank said.

"I know he was a wildman back then, and sometimes he turns nasty now, but underneath he's really just a big teddy bear. He's helped my family so much we'll never be able to repay him. I refuse to believe he could ever deliberately do anything to hurt someone. If you really want to get to the bottom of this, keep your eyes on McCracken and his crowd."

"That's exactly what we're doing," Joe said.

Natalie squinted at the younger Hardy out of the corner of her eye. "You just went BASE jumping with them, didn't you?"

"Unless you've got a better idea," Frank said, "it's the only way to find out what's going on."

"Just be careful," Natalie said. "Fixed object jumping's dangerous enough without having to do it with a bunch of raving lunatics."

"Don't worry," Joe said. "We'll be extra cautious. We'll double-check our gear, and we won't jump if there's any doubt about the conditions."

"Sure," Natalie said. "Anyway, if you need any pointers, let me know."

"Sounds like you've done a bit of BASE jumping yourself," Frank said.

"I've been known to jump off a cliff or two in my time," Natalie admitted. "But not anymore—especially not after what happened to Kurt." She glanced at her watch. "I've got to get going. My mother'll be worried if I'm not home soon."

The brothers walked Natalie to her car and said good night. Then they went back to their van and climbed in. Joe put the key in the ignition but didn't start it. He turned to his brother. "I still don't understand why anyone would rig someone's chute to malfunction."

"It might be a good way to keep someone quiet," Frank suggested with a shrug.

"True." Joe yawned. "I'm bushed. Let's go home and get some sleep."

Just then they saw Dave Shima crossing the other side of the lot to a small red sports car. "I thought he already went home with the rest of them," Joe said.

"Apparently not," Frank said. "I guess we'll just have to catch up on our sleep some other time."

Joe fired up the van and rolled out of the lot behind Shima's car. He left the headlights off as they followed Shima to Squirrel McCracken's house. Parked a few houses away, he and Frank watched Shima go to the front door. A moment later Squirrel came out, and the two began to talk on the front porch.

Frank and Joe eased themselves out of the van and sneaked behind a hedge next to the Mc-Cracken house. At first Shima and McCracken were talking too quietly to be heard, but soon Shima raised his voice. "You're going to have to come up with the money or drop out, Squirrel."

"I'll have the five hundred soon," McCracken said.

"Everybody else is paid up."

"I told you I'll get the money." McCracken looked around. "Keep it down, Dave. Do you want to wake up the neighbors?"

"I don't care about the neighbors," Shima said.

"Then why don't you shut up and get out of here," McCracken said.

Shima took a step toward McCracken. "Watch how you talk to me."

"I said get out of my face." McCracken gave Shima a shove.

With startling speed Shima whipped around, catching McCracken in the chest with his left foot. McCracken fell against a column at the corner of the porch. When Shima came at him, McCracken kicked out with both feet and slammed him against the front door. Shima grunted in pain.

"We should break this up," Joe whispered to his brother.

"Hold it," Frank said. "Let's not blow our cover so fast."

Shima jabbed McCracken hard in the chest with an elbow, then gave him an expert karate chop to the back of his neck. McCracken sank to one knee, then suddenly lurched up, driving his shoulder into Shima's midsection. The blow sent Shima flying off the porch, straight at the spot where Joe was crouching behind the hedge.

Chapter

9

SHIMA CAME CRASHING into the hedge, flopped over, and landed on top of Joe before Joe could scramble clear. They were both stunned for a moment, but Shima bounced to his feet first. He squared off against Joe and shouted, "Hey, what're you two doing hiding down here?"

"None of your business," Joe said. "We were just—"

Frank started toward Shima, who must have thought it was an attack, because he suddenly jabbed his right foot at Frank's head. Ready for the blow, Frank snagged Shima's foot inches from his face and twisted it, forcing him back to the ground. Still holding the foot, Frank drew back his own, ready to thrust it into Shima's stomach.

Shima threw up his hands. "All right, all right. Enough."

Frank let go of Shima and went over to his brother. "Joe, are you okay?"

"Fine," Joe said. "I guess I was just a step slow after he clobbered me."

Frank turned in time to see McCracken start toward Shima, who was still on the ground. "Hold it right there, McCracken," Frank warned.

Having seen Frank's karate display, McCracken stopped in his tracks, giving Shima a chance to get to his feet.

"What were you two fighting about?" Joe said.

"That's none of *your* business," McCracken said defiantly. "By the way, where did you guys come from? I didn't hear you drive up."

Joe thought fast. "We were on our way home when we saw you two going at it. You didn't notice us."

McCracken thought about this for a moment. "Well, it's still none of your business," he said. "Now, why don't you two just clear out?" He turned, climbed up the front steps, and went inside the house, slamming the door behind him.

Shima went to his car, and the Hardys headed back to their van. Before they got in, though, Shima called after them, "Frank, Joe." They stopped. "Can I buy you guys a cup of coffee?"

"Sure," Frank said.

Joe climbed into the back of Shima's car while Frank slipped into the shotgun seat. Shima drove them to an all-night diner a few blocks away. They sat at a booth by a window overlooking the street and ordered coffee and pie.

"What's this all about?" Joe asked.

Shima dug his fork into a piece of pie. "Squirrel, Silk, and I came up with this idea for a contest a couple of weeks ago. We picked ten BASE jumps in the New York City area." He ticked them off. "There's the World Trade Center, the Verrazano Narrows Bridge, the George Washington Bridge, the Empire State Building, the New Jersey Palisades, the UN building, Thirty Rockefeller Plaza . . . I'm forgetting a few. The WZZM radio tower out in Jersey . . ."

Joe interrupted him. "So you were the ones who jumped off WZZM?"

"Yep, that was us you saw on the news," Shima admitted with obvious pride. "If you want in on the contest, you'll have to make up that jump, along with Metrocorp."

"Is the Chrysler Building on the list?" Frank said.

"Sure. The bad news is the rest of us are a couple jumps ahead of you, but the good news is you only have nine left to go."

"I can't speak for both of us," Frank said, "but considering the risks, I'm not sure it's worth it just for a few thrills."

A sly smile crept across Shima's face. "I haven't mentioned the best part. We're each chipping in five hundred bucks toward a grand prize of ten thousand, winner take all."

"But if you're all jumping together," Joe said, "what kind of contest is that?"

"You never know what's going to happen on a BASE jump," Shima said. "Someone could drop out, someone could get injured. . . . Once we get down to the last few jumps, I'm sure it'll be a free-for-all. Plus if two more join, the prize is eleven grand. What do you say?"

"How do you know somebody hasn't already done some jumps on his own and taken a lead?" Frank said.

"We don't," Shima said. "It's all part of the contest, planning the jumps and being the first one to pull off all ten. Of course, I wouldn't recommend doing *all* of them by yourself."

"How do you verify the jumps if there's no one else there?" Joe asked.

"Videotape, eyewitness reports, a news story," Shima said. "As long as the judges agree."

"Who are they?" Joe said.

"I really can't say right now."

"So what if it's a tie?" Frank said.

"Sudden-death tiebreaker," Shima said. "No pun intended, but the first one to make another jump wins. So, are you in or not?"

"Five hundred bucks for the pool?" Frank said. "That's a lot of money."

"Personally I don't keep that much cash just lying around," Joe said.

"Neither do I," Frank said. "But I'm sure we can find a way to scrape it together."

"When and where is the next jump?" Joe asked.

"We'll let you know," Shima said. "Meanwhile, don't let any of us stop you from jumping on your own."

When they finished, Shima drove Frank and Joe back to their van, then he took off.

"Did you hear that?" Joe said. "Shima admitted the Metrocorp was part of the contest, which proves they were the guys with Kurt Waller the night he died."

"Sure," Frank said, "but would it hold up in court? Shima didn't say when they jumped off the Metrocorp or who was with them. And we still don't know that the death wasn't an accident."

Joe guided the van onto the main highway toward Bayport. They drove for a few minutes in silence until Frank said, "Something's bugging me about this contest."

"What's that?" Joe asked.

"There were five jumpers before we came along, six if you count Kurt Waller, right?"

"Yeah, so?"

"If each of them is putting up five hundred bucks, how could the prize be ten thousand dollars? It doesn't add up."

"Do you think maybe Squirrel and Dave were hoping nobody would notice?" Joe asked.

"I don't think any of them are that dumb. I'm thinking maybe there's someone else involved—someone who isn't jumping."

"Could somebody like Kritzer be sponsoring it?" Joe said.

"Sure," Frank said. "But the question is why?"

The next morning Frank and Joe wolfed down an early breakfast and drove directly to JFK International. They got to Bob Edgewater's office well before seven. Shirley Bascombe, his assistant, was already there. She offered them coffee, and they restlessly read aviation magazines until Edgewater finally arrived.

"Frank, Joe, good morning," the FAA investigator said as he led them inside his smaller office. He threw his overcoat onto the sofa and sat behind his desk. "What brings you here so bright and early?"

"We've got some more information on the BASE jumpers out at Ridgeway," Frank said as he and Joe took seats across from Edgewater.

"This wouldn't have anything to do with last night's jump off the Chrysler Building, would it?"

Joe squirmed in his seat, not sure how Edgewater was going to react to their involvement. "Yes, we were there."

"That was a dangerous stunt," Edgewater said. "I'm glad no one was hurt."

"But that's only part of it," Frank said. "They started a contest: the first one to jump from ten

95

predetermined spots will win ten grand. Each of them is kicking in five hundred dollars."

Edgewater whistled. "That's a lot of money. If my math is correct, it means there are twenty jumpers involved."

"There are only five," Joe said.

Edgewater frowned. "Hmm. Bad math."

"We think they have a sponsor," Frank said. "We're trying to figure out who it could be."

"They asked us to join the contest," Joe said. "It would be a great way to keep an eye on them, but we need to come up with the money."

"I think I can pull a thousand out of petty cash, especially since you've done such a good job so far. Any idea when and where the next jump is?"

"No," Frank said. "But they did tell us some of the other sites." He listed them while Edgewater wrote them down.

"They also admitted to the Metrocorp jump and the one off the WZZM radio tower," Joe added.

The investigator studied the list. "It appears that you two are going to be busy. I want you to know that no one expects you to participate in these jumps."

"We want to see this one through to the end," Frank said. He turned to Joe. "Which reminds me, I'd better call Mr. Waller and give him an update."

Joe nodded. "By the way," he said to Edgewater, "we've got a couple more names for you to run through the computer."

"Give me a minute to get on-line." Swiveling around in his chair to face the computer next to his desk, Edgewater worked the keyboard. "Okay," he said, "fire away."

"Dave Shima and Squirrel McCracken," Joe said.

"You're jumping with somebody named Squirrel?" Edgewater said, his eyebrows shooting up.

"It's his nickname," Frank said. "His real name is Kenny. He's sort of the ringleader."

Edgewater typed D. SHIMA into the computer and waited while the Hardys looked over his shoulder. A few seconds later the screen read: NO RECORDS MATCH REQUEST. "Nothing on Shima," he said. He typed in K. MCCRACKEN and waited. Half a minute later entries began filling the screen. "Bingo! Squirrel's been a busy boy. He's been cited for jumping through clouds, jumping after dark, creating a disturbance during a flight, refusing to show his license, jumping without a license. Nothing really sinister, but he's definitely been a problem."

He turned away from the screen. "I'll run Shima through some other databases. It'll take a while, though. I'll let you know what turns up."

"Thanks, inspector," Frank said.

"By the way, nice job infiltrating this group, Shirley," he called. When she appeared at the door, he asked, "Would you please give these

97

gentlemen a thousand dollars from the cash drawer?"

"Right away, sir."

"Keep up the good work," Edgewater said as the Hardys got up from their seats.

Edgewater's assistant counted out twenty fifty-dollars bills and handed them to Frank. "Don't let them fall out of your pocket," she warned.

"Thanks, I'll button them up extra tight," Frank said.

It was still early when the Hardys arrived at Ridgeway Airport. Most of the employees were at the Drop Inn having breakfast. There were a few people manning the commuter airline counter, but the rest of the airport seemed deserted.

Joe spotted a plane he hadn't seen before parked by the runway. "Isn't that one of those experimental jets we've been reading about in the magazines?" he asked.

"I think so," Frank said. "Let's check it out."

As they headed toward the sleek new plane, Frank heard a loud bang inside the Wild Blue Yonder's hangar. "Did you hear that?"

"Yeah," Joe said. "Probably just someone working on one of the planes."

They heard another bang, followed by a crash, and Frank shook his head. "That doesn't sound right."

As the banging continued, he jogged to the

hangar's side door. He peered inside and saw Spencer Johnson swinging a four-foot-long crowbar at Tomcat Kritzer's Cessna. Its fuselage was already badly dented.

"Spencer, stop it!" Frank yelled.

Johnson swung the huge crowbar in a wide arc and smashed it into one of the plane's windows, shattering the glass into tiny shards that sprayed all over.

"Get out of here, kid," Johnson said, "or I'll crush *you*." Then he whacked the bar down on one of the plane's wings, rupturing its tank and splashing fuel onto the concrete floor.

"Tomcat ruined my life," Johnson shouted. "Now I'm going to ruin his!"

"Just stop it," Frank said. He put his hand on Johnson's shoulder, but the old fighter pilot spun around and swung the bar straight at his head.

Chapter

10

JOE CHARGED IN behind Frank and went for Johnson's arms, but before he got there Johnson spun out on the aviation fuel. He missed Frank wildly and went down, hitting his head on the plane's wing and knocking himself out cold.

Joe bent over the old flyer as Frank knelt to feel his wrist. "He's got a pulse, but we better call nine-one-one just to be safe," Frank said.

Joe scrambled to his feet and ran to a wall phone next to the door. Within seconds the emergency operator assured him that help was on the way. Meanwhile, Johnson opened his eyes, sputtered, and gazed up at Frank. "What happened?" he said.

"You passed out," Frank answered. "Just lie still. We've called for help."

Tomcat Kritzer appeared at the door followed by a few of his students. "What's going on here?" he said. Then he saw the damaged Cessna and a look of utter shock crossed his face. "Who did this?"

"We found Spencer going after it with a crowbar," Joe said.

Kritzer took a look at the dented fuselage, then lunged toward Johnson. Joe grabbed him by the arm and said, "You have every right to be mad. But I think he might have a concussion."

Kritzer backed off, his face red and chest heaving. "The old fool!" he spat out. "He should have gotten out of this business a long time ago." Kritzer kicked a nearby trash can and uttered a curse.

A siren outside announced the emergency van. A moment later two paramedics hurried in carrying a first aid kit and an oxygen tank. Natalie followed them in and rushed to Johnson's side. Frank and Joe stood by until Johnson, an oxygen mask strapped to his face, was wheeled out to the ambulance on a gurney.

Joe saw the worried look on Natalie's face as she watched the ambulance leave the airport. He asked her if she needed a ride to the hospital. She shook her head. "He's in good hands now. Besides, somebody's going to have to mind the store."

"Let us know if you need any help," Frank said.

"Thanks, guys," Natalie said. The brothers watched her walk slowly back to Johnson's hangar.

When Frank was certain she was out of earshot, he said to Joe, "If we had any doubts about Johnson wanting to get revenge for what Tomcat did, those doubts are now gone."

"But I still have my doubts that Johnson had anything to do with Kurt Waller's death," Joe said. "I just don't get the connection, do you?"

Frank had to admit he didn't. "Maybe if we present the Leaping Lizards with some cash, they'll talk a little more," he suggested.

"It's worth a shot," Joe said.

Later Frank and Joe made a few conventional jumps from one of the Wild Blue Yonder's planes. After their leap from the Chrysler Building, free-falling from thirteen thousand feet into an open field seemed like child's play, even on a windy day. To keep things interesting the brothers worked on their landing techniques.

"Whoever lands farthest from the center of the drop zone buys lunch," Joe said to Frank over the roar of the plane. They were sitting alongside several other skydivers on their fourth jump of the day.

"You're on," Frank said.

When they flew over the drop zone, Joe leaped out of the plane, hugged his knees up to his chin, and somersaulted over and over. Not to be outdone, Frank dove headfirst after him, passing Joe well before they deployed their chutes.

Manipulating his control lines expertly, Frank landed within a few yards of the drop zone bull's-eye. A minute later Joe looked as though he was going to miss the target altogether. But at the last second he managed to ride out a gust of wind and maneuver himself directly over the target. His landing was as smooth as if he were stepping off a curb.

Joe let out a loud whoop. "Somebody owes his younger, better-looking brother lunch," he said, reining in his chute.

"What do you mean, 'better-looking'?" Frank said. "Let's try another couple of jumps and see who looks better."

"No way. I'm starving."

"Okay," Frank said, "but after lunch I'm pulling out all the stops."

They rode the bus back to the airport, and then slipped into a booth at the Drop Inn. Joe had just polished off his first burger and was about to tackle another when Squirrel came in, followed by Silk and the others. They joined the Hardys.

"You boys seen this?" Squirrel asked, throwing a folded newspaper down on the table.

Frank looked at it. "It's the newspaper. What's the big deal?"

Silk burst into a grin. "Open it," he said.

Frank spread the paper out on the table, seeing that it was a local edition. The headline read, "Six

Make Daring Late-Night Leap from Chrysler Building." He read out loud, " 'At approximately ten o'clock last night, six young men wearing parachutes jumped from the sixty-first floor of the Chrysler Building into the city streets below. Responding to calls from several eyewitnesses, police arrived on the scene within minutes, but were too late to make any arrests.' "

"Don't you love it?" Silk said.

"I'm amazed they ran it on the front page," Joe said.

"Must have been a slow news day," Frank said.

"Slow my foot," Squirrel said. "Nobody's ever done that."

"I have to admit," Joe said, "it was one of the most exciting things I've ever done."

"You bet it was," Silk said.

Dave Shima appeared calmer than his friends. He looked from one Hardy to the other. "So, did you guys come up with the money?"

Frank took out the plain envelope containing the cash Bob Edgewater had given them and handed it to Shima. Without opening it, Shima handed the envelope to Silk. "Randall's going to hold on to the money until there's a winner. Welcome aboard." He extended his hand to Frank and Joe.

The rest of the group had a quick lunch. When he was through, Squirrel pushed away his empty plate. "That was good. Now, are you lizards ready to jump off a bridge?"

"You know we are," Silk said.

"All right," Shima said. "Then let's roll."

Frank, Joe, and the five other jumpers drove west in Silk Randall's van with Shima behind the wheel. Soon the skyline of Manhattan came into view. Joe could barely make out the Chrysler Building through the early-afternoon haze. It was hard for him to believe that only the night before he and Frank had jumped off one of the world's tallest buildings. And now they were going do it again from a bridge. But which one?

His question was answered when Shima took the Belt Parkway to Brooklyn and they saw the Verrazano Narrows Bridge, the world's longest single-span suspension bridge, come into view.

"Okay, here's the plan," Silk said. "Everybody gear up now in the van. Dave's going to pull over and drop us at the base of the east tower. We take the stairs to the top. Meanwhile, he crosses the bridge, pulls a U-turn, then comes back and waits onshore—there's a little park down by the water there. We land close to the van and get going."

They all took turns getting ready in the back of the van as it got closer to its destination. Frank was putting on his helmet when he saw Silk's lying upside-down on the floor. Something inside it caught his eye. In the interior of the helmet, at the back, was a tiny black box. A black cable ran along the inside of the helmet to the front, where it barely poked out beside the dark visor.

"Hey, Frank," someone said.

Startled, Frank looked up to see Randall staring directly at him. "Yeah, Silk."

"Better get the lead out. We're almost there."

"I'm with you," Frank said as Shima pulled over at the base of the tower. They all hopped out, hurtling over the guardrail and huddling by a door at the base of the tower.

"Keep an eye out for bridge workers or cops," Squirrel said as he started to pick the lock on the tower door.

"Awesome," Joe said, glancing up at the tower.

"It's six hundred ninety feet on top of that thing," Rush said. "More than a thousand stairs. Luckily we're already partway up."

Once Squirrel had the door open, they hurried inside and Silk led the way up the stairs, setting a fast pace. With all the equipment on their backs, however, they soon slowed down.

Rush was the first to stop. "How much farther?" he gasped.

Kamikaze came up from the rear. "Oh, man, we're not even halfway there yet."

"You sound more like weeping wimps than leaping lizards," Squirrel said. "Anyone who doesn't want to make the climb can bail now."

There were several groans, but when Squirrel started climbing again, everyone followed. Joe was starting to feel it in his legs when they finally made it to the top after about fifteen minutes of fast climbing. They stepped onto the steel platform and checked out the view. The New York skyline looked small in the distance. They could see the yellow van parked near the water way below. The wind was blowing something fierce.

"This should be interesting." Squirrel stepped to the edge and looked down. "All right, guys, the two things we don't want to do are land in the water or on the roadway. Silk, you first."

Silk adjusted his helmet, checked his harness, and stepped to the edge of the platform. "See you Lizards at the bottom," he said. With that he bent his knees and gave a powerful push, diving as far out from the tower as he could. The rest of the jumpers watched his chute open and saw him drift first out over the water, then back toward the shore. Rush went next, with Kamikaze, Frank, and Joe right behind him. They gathered their chutes quickly after landing, then stood on the grass to watch Squirrel make his jump.

"Why's he taking so long?" Frank asked.

Silk snorted. "He probably wants to make sure we're all down here watching. Nobody loves having an audience more than Squirrel."

Squirrel jumped away from the bridge and pulled his rip cord almost immediately.

"He's going to ride this one out as long as he can," Shima said.

They watched him turn and drift over the roadway. He cleared the bridge's cables by only a few feet.

"That was close," Rush said.

Squirrel circled behind the tower and out of sight. When he came around, he was doing his best to steer toward the shore, but all of a sudden he began to drift sideways.

"The wind got him," Silk said. "He's heading for those rocks."

Squirrel was falling fast toward a jetty of jagged rocks that jutted into the narrows. He managed to veer away from the rocks just in time, but the wind carried him back out and he splashed down a hundred yards from shore. He thrashed around in the choppy water for a few seconds, then disappeared under the waves.

"He's tangled in his lines," Joe said as Squirrel's head bobbed to the surface once more.

He disappeared again, and, seeing that he didn't resurface, Frank shouted, "He's going down. We have to save him!"

Chapter

11

FRANK AND JOE RAN to the shoreline, pulled off their helmets, jumpsuits, and shoes, and dived in. They swam fast toward where Squirrel was struggling to surface. Joe's legs were cramping up on him in the frigid water. Every kick was painful, but he pressed on right behind Frank.

Just before they got to Squirrel, he went under again. Frank dived down and grabbed him. Joe tried to free the chute lines, but they were too tangled. He was starting to unhitch Squirrel's harness when Frank whipped out his pocketknife and started cutting. Though Joe's fingers were numb, he grabbed Squirrel and held on tight to stop the jumper's blind thrashing.

"Relax, Squirrel," Joe shouted, trying not to

109

swallow too much water. He managed to turn Squirrel over on his back and started hauling him toward shore. Frank relieved him at the halfway point. When they finally reached the shoreline, the other jumpers pulled Squirrel out of the water and carried him over the rocks to softer ground.

"He needs CPR," Frank yelled. He and Joe were too cold and exhausted to do it themselves.

"I got it," Shima said. He checked Squirrel's windpipe for obstructions, then used both hands to pump his chest. He gave Squirrel mouth-to-mouth resuscitation, repeating the procedure three times until Squirrel started coughing up water.

"Kamikaze, get some blankets or something from the van," Joe said. Squirrel sat up, sputtering and shivering.

Kamikaze ran to the van and returned with a blanket and every piece of clothing he could find. He draped the blanket around Squirrel's shoulders and tossed jackets and sweaters to Frank and Joe.

"Are you okay?" Frank asked Squirrel.

Squirrel got unsteadily to his feet and threw off the blanket. "Ready to do it all over again."

"I don't think so," Joe said.

"You ought to get checked out by a doctor," Frank said.

"I'm telling you I'm fine," Squirrel protested. He looked down at the cut lines dangling from

110

his harness. "Hey," he said, "what happened to my chute?"

"We had to slice the lines to get you out of the water," Frank explained.

"Who told you to do that?" Squirrel said.

"Sorry, Squirrel," Joe said, "but Frank didn't have any choice. You were drowning."

"You messed up my best chute," Squirrel said. "I oughta—"

Shima stepped between them. "Don't be ridiculous. You should be thanking the Hardys for saving your life."

"It's true," Rush added.

Squirrel looked around at the other jumpers, who nodded back. He thought for a few moments. "In that case, thanks," he finally said, and shook Frank's hand.

"All right now, let's get out of here before the cops show up," Silk said.

It was dark by the time Silk dropped Frank and Joe back at Ridgeway Airport. They waved good night to the others and climbed into their van. "I can't wait to get home," Joe said as he started the engine. "I'm going to eat a big hot dinner and hit the sack fast."

"Sounds good," Frank said. "But there's something I want to check out before we go home." He turned the ignition off.

"What's so important it can't wait till tomorrow?"

"When Silk put his helmet down this afternoon I noticed some kind of electronic device inside."

"What was it?" Joe asked.

"There was this cable about a half inch around that ran from the front of the helmet to a couple of black boxes at the back. They were maybe three inches square and no more than an inch thick."

"Doesn't sound like anything I've heard of," Joe said.

They waited in their van until Shima and the others dropped their gear in the Wild Blue Yonder locker room and drove off. Then Frank and Joe quietly crossed the parking lot to the locker room door, which was bathed in the light of a security lamp directly overhead.

Frank tried the doorknob. "Locked."

Joe pulled out his lock-picking set and went to work. Within moments, they were inside. Frank shone his penlight around at the rows of lockers. He stopped at the one with T. Randall scrawled on a piece of tape on the door. In addition to its built-in combination lock, Silk had placed a heavy padlock on the door.

"Extra security," Joe observed.

"Which tells me he's probably got something more valuable than just jump gear stowed inside," Frank said.

"Either that or he's paranoid." Joe had the padlock off in an instant. The combination lock, however, took good ears and a steady hand. Three minutes later Joe had the locker open.

"Here it is," Frank said. He plucked Randall's helmet from the top shelf, turned it over, and showed Joe the inside with the little boxes and cable. "What do you make of it?"

"Beats me," Joe said. "Let's take it to Phil and see what he thinks."

They took the helmet back to their van and headed to Phil Cohen's house. Once they got there, they went in the back door and up to Phil's room. Phil sat hunched over one of his computers amid the scores of other electronic devices that took up just about every square inch of space.

"Hi, guys," he said without looking up from the screen. "I'm on-line with a person in Singapore who says he can get me an incredible deal on one of the fastest RAM chips made." He tapped a few keys, then looked up. "He's just sending me the specs now."

"Can you tell us what this is?" Frank said, handing him Silk's helmet.

Phil turned the helmet around under a lamp with a magnifying glass built into it and looked at it from all angles. His eyes grew wide as he studied the end of the cable that stuck out of the helmet. "Well, I'll be," he said. "I never thought I'd see one of these."

"What is it, Phil?" Joe said.

"One of the most remarkable examples of miniaturization in existence." Phil put his index

113

finger on one of the black boxes. "Gentlemen, this has got to be the world's tiniest video camera." He pointed to the end of the cable. "That's a lens. The image passes through this optical fiber."

Joe studied the small black boxes. "You mean there's a little videotape in there, something we could play back if we had the right equipment?"

"Not quite," Phil replied. "It's too small for that. I figure this other black box houses a transmitter that sends pictures to a recorder at another location."

"I wonder where Silk keeps the receiver and the recorder," Frank said.

"Maybe hidden in his jumpsuit," Joe said.

"Impossible," Phil said. "They'd be too big."

"How far do you think the camera could transmit?" Joe asked.

"About a half mile, maybe a mile tops."

Frank snapped his fingers. "It's probably mounted somewhere in that yellow van of his."

"How do you know so much about these cameras if you've never actually seen one?" Joe asked Phil.

"I've been reading about them on the Internet. The FBI and the CIA have been using them for surveillance. There aren't too many of them and they're definitely worth serious bucks."

Frank frowned. "How would a skydiver be able to afford something like this, let alone get his hands on one? And why bother?" Frank went on. "Why not just use a regular helmet-mounted video cam like Shima does for the skysurfing?"

"Secrecy," Joe said. "I think we need to stick close to Mr. Randall and find out what he's really up to."

"And who's bankrolling him," Frank added. He picked up the helmet.

Phil gazed longingly at the miniature camera. "I sure wish you could leave it with me for a while. I'd really like to take it apart and see what makes it tick."

"Sorry," Frank said. "We've got to get it back into Silk's locker before he notices it's gone."

"When you do find the recorder," Phil said as the Hardys headed for the door, "I'd sure like to have a look at that, too."

"You mean, *if* we find it," Joe said. "Thanks for the analysis." He and Frank headed for the door.

"Wait a second," Phil said. "Have you seen my new parabolic mike?"

"We don't have time for that right now, Phil," Frank said.

"But it's really cool," Phil said, jumping to his feet. He plucked a box from a stack of crates, opened it, and pulled out what looked like a miniature satellite dish.

"You've got lots of parabolics," Joe said. "What's so special about this one?"

"It's way smaller, and it's also digital. I can

pick up somebody whispering at four hundred yards."

Joe looked at Frank. "Might be just what we need to eavesdrop on Silk."

"Mind if we borrow it, Phil?" Joe said.

"As long as I go along with it," Phil said.

"No way," Joe said.

"Why should you guys have all the fun?" Phil protested. "You want my mike, you get me, too. Besides, you don't know how to work it."

"All right," Frank said, "but this could get hairy. So if we tell you to leave, you leave."

"It's a deal," Phil said. "Let's move out." He carefully placed the microphone in a padded canvas bag, slung it over his shoulder, and followed the Hardys out to their van.

They made a quick stop at Ridgeway Municipal Airport to put Silk's helmet back in his locker, then headed over to his apartment complex. It was after eleven o'clock by the time they rolled up in front.

"I wonder which unit is his," Joe said.

"Let's check the mailboxes," Frank said.

"I'll do it," Phil said.

"That might not be such a good idea," Joe said.

"Look, even if he sees me, he has no idea who I am," Phil pointed out. "Come to think of it, I have no idea who he is, either. What's his name?"

"Randall," Frank said. "Timothy Randall, also known as Silk."

Phil hopped out of the van and walked across the street to the building's entrance. The Hardys watched him scan the mailboxes, then go inside. After ten minutes of checking his watch, Joe started to worry. "What's keeping him?" he said. "He should have been back ages ago. We'd better go in after him."

"Just a second—" Frank said, but Joe was already climbing out of the van. Frank followed him to the building and they checked the mailboxes, then headed up to Randall's apartment, number 3A.

Rounding the corner at the top of the stairs, they saw Phil striding toward them. When he saw them, he motioned frantically with his hand for them to turn back.

Joe stopped with Frank right behind. A door swung open down the hall and Joe heard Silk say, "Hey, Phil, that must be your friends right now."

Oh, no, Joe thought, quickly spinning around to hide. We've blown our cover!

Chapter

12

FRANK AND JOE DUCKED BACK onto the staircase. "Do you think he saw us?" Joe whispered. Frank motioned for him to be quiet.

"Thanks for the directions, Silk," Phil said in a loud voice. "Sorry to bother you."

"Okay, Phil, you take care," Silk said, and slammed the door.

"Come on, guys, let's get out of here," Phil hissed. "That was close."

When they got back to the van, Phil said, "You two almost got me into a major mess back there."

"What happened in there?" Frank asked.

"I had a nice chat with your buddy, Mr. Timothy 'Silk' Randall."

"You took an awfully long time," Joe said.

"We got worried so we went in to see what was taking you so long."

"Not to worry," Phil said with a self-satisfied smile. "I had it all under control. I just played dumb and told him my friends and I were looking for the Petersons. They live upstairs. I rang their bell first to make sure they weren't home. It gave me a chance to scope out Silk's apartment for the video recorder and receiver."

"Not bad, Phil," Frank said. "Did you see anything?"

"No. But I do know the perfect place to set up the parabolic mike."

"Where?" Frank and Joe said together.

"Drive around back. I'll show you."

Joe drove the van down an unlit alley that ran behind the building.

"Silk's in the apartment next to the garage," Phil said. He pulled out the parabolic mike, put on a pair of headphones, and adjusted the amplifier so Frank and Joe could hear. "Pull forward a few feet so I can get a better angle."

Joe rolled the van ahead until Randall came into view through the narrow space between the garage and the building next door. He was sitting on the couch in his living room watching television. Frank, Joe, and Phil heard the TV as clearly as if they were in the room with him. They could even hear the crunching of the potato chips he was eating from a bowl on his lap. For almost an hour they watched him do this.

119

Phil yawned. "This is exciting. Now we know what TV shows he watches and that he likes to eat potato chips."

Frank turned to Phil. "Welcome to the typical stakeout. You spend days tailing a suspect and all you find out is how boring his life really is."

"Then sometimes you get lucky," Joe said.

Phil yawned again. "Let's hope we get lucky tonight." He leaned back against the headrest and dozed off.

Forty-five minutes later the phone in Randall's apartment rang, bringing the three of them to attention.

Randall answered on the second ring. "Hello. You're late." All they could hear in the van was a muffled reply.

"Can't you tune that thing so we can hear the caller?" Joe asked.

Phil adjusted the dials on the mike's amplifier. Shaking his head, he said, "Sorry. He's got the phone pressed too tightly to his ear."

Randall spoke again. "The figure sounds right, but we're going to need some money up front." He listened for a beat, then said, "At least twenty percent down to show good faith."

There was another pause, then Randall said, "Where?" and scribbled something on a note pad.

"Can't you make it earlier, say, one?" Silk listened again, then said, "Good. We'll meet you there at one-thirty." He nodded. "Right. I'll be at the airport all morning if you need to get hold of me. 'Bye.''

Randall hung up the phone and stretched, then turned off the TV and the lights. All Frank and Joe could hear was some shuffling in the apartment, followed by silence.

"What do you think that phone call was all about?" Phil asked after a few minutes.

"Hard to tell," Joe said. "A deal is definitely going down tomorrow afternoon, but for all we know he could be selling a few parachutes."

"On the other hand," Frank said, "he might have been talking about the BASE-jumping contest. I say we stick to Silk."

Joe agreed.

"I'm with you guys," Phil said.

"Great, Phil," Frank said. "You can help us follow Silk around tomorrow. We'll probably be doing some jumping, and we'd love to have you along."

"Jumping?" Phil said. "On second thought, maybe I should sit this one out."

Joe laughed as he started up the engine.

"So, we can have your mike without you tomorrow?" Frank asked.

"You can have it," Phil said. "I'll show you how it works."

Frank and Joe drove out to the Ridgeway airport bright and early the next morning. Squirrel, Silk, Kamikaze, and Rush were going up with boards to practice for another skysurfing competition, which was coming up in a couple of weeks. Dave Shima wore his conventional camera helmet and the jumpsuit with batlike wings to control his descent speed. Also among the jumpers waiting to board the first plane of the day was Natalie. She sat by herself on a bench outside the hangar with her nose buried in a book.

"I'm going over to say hello," Joe said.

"Go ahead," Frank said, "but she doesn't look like she wants company right now."

Ignoring Frank, Joe approached Natalie. "Hi, Nat. Great day for jumping, huh?"

She shrugged her shoulders. "To tell you the truth, I hadn't even noticed."

"Mind if I sit?" Joe asked.

"Suit yourself," she said without looking up. "It's not my bench."

"Sorry about what happened to Spencer."

"It was bound to happen sooner or later. He's always been his own worst enemy."

"How's he doing?"

"Well, he gave himself a mild heart attack, but that's under control with medication. He's already roaring around, making the nurses on his floor miserable."

Joe smiled. "I'm glad to hear it. Any idea what brought all that on?"

"You haven't heard?" Natalie asked.

Joe shook his head.

"The night before the attack Spencer found out the bank was closing down his school. He hasn't been making the payments on his loan. I guess he got himself pretty worked up and just exploded."

"I'm sorry, Nat. Have you started looking for another job?"

"Not yet. After working here, skydiving, and fixing up planes, I'm not too big on the idea of bagging groceries at the supermarket."

"I'm sure you could get work as an instructor. Have you talked to Tomcat yet?"

Natalie's eyes flashed with anger. "I'd quit jumping for good before I went to work for that creep. Spencer may not have managed the academy very well, but Kritzer put the last nail in its coffin." She looked around to make sure they weren't being overheard. "How's your investigation going?"

"We're making some progress," Joe said. "We should know a lot more by this afternoon."

"Keep me informed, okay?" Natalie said.

"I promise you'll be the first to know."

"First to know what?" Joe and Natalie were surprised to see Squirrel standing in front of them.

"About whether I buy this new canopy shell she recommended," Joe said.

"Oh," Squirrel said, turning to Natalie. "You going up?"

"Yeah," Natalie answered. "Why?"

"Darcy's about to take off in the Twin Otter."

Joe and Natalie gathered up their equipment and boarded the plane with the others.

Once they were airborne, Silk handed Frank

two skysurfing boards. He shouted to him over the roar of the plane's engines, "Let's see what you and Joe can do with these strapped to your feet."

"Thanks," Frank shouted back. He handed one of the boards to his brother. Joe gave Silk a thumbs-up.

Over the drop zone, Joe jumped with the board. Since it felt to him a lot like snowboarding, which he was good at, he tried a flip like the ones he'd seen Squirrel and the others doing. He immediately lost control. But unlike snowboarding, there wasn't any snow to plant his face in. He caught his balance and tried a spin.

Frank, on the other hand, decided to get used to the feel of his board slowly. He found that by tipping it only slightly he could shoot off in any direction, as if he were dropping down the face of a huge wave. It was hard to believe he was falling toward the earth at well over one hundred miles an hour.

Frank and Joe made another couple of jumps, keeping an eye on Silk Randall the entire time. Everyone broke at noon for lunch at the Drop Inn. After gobbling down his sandwich, Frank pushed away his plate and got to his feet. "Come on, Joe," he said. Joe crammed the last of his french fries in his mouth and stood up, wondering why Frank was so rushed.

"Where are you two going?" Squirrel asked.

"We're picking up a modem for our dad's computer," Frank said. "Not that it's any of your business."

"You might want to be back before two-thirty," Silk said. "We've got another 'event' planned for this afternoon." He winked at them.

"We'll be back in time," Joe said. The brothers walked out of the Drop Inn and headed across the parking lot to their van.

"Weren't we going to stick with Silk?" Joe said.

"We are. But I didn't want to be too obvious about it." He pointed to a storage building by the entrance to the airport. "Let's wait behind that shed until he takes off."

"Good thinking," Joe said as they climbed into their van.

Fifteen minutes later Frank and Joe watched from their van as Silk left the Drop Inn. He got into his van and pulled out of the parking lot. Joe tailed him until he pulled into a wooded park on the far edge of town and parked out of sight. Slinging the case with the parabolic mike over his shoulder, Frank started out the door. He stopped at the sound of a voice from the back of the van.

"Wait," Natalie said. "I'm coming with you."

"Nat!" Joe exclaimed. "What are you doing back there?"

She climbed over the seats to the front. "I really wanted to find out what was going on, so I sneaked in here and waited while you were stuffing your faces at the Drop Inn."

"Come on," Frank said. "We're going to lose him."

"Nat, you wait here," Joe said.

Natalie was defiant. "No way I'm staying behind."

Frank glanced at her, then said, "All right, but promise to be quiet and keep out of sight."

"Excuse me, but I can do that at least as well as the two of you," she said. "You didn't even know I was in the van all this time." Joe had to admit that she had a point.

The three of them climbed out of the van and began running in the direction they had last seen Randall. They followed him to a meadow surrounded by dense woods. From the cover of the trees, they watched Randall approach a woman in the middle of the meadow.

"Who's that?" Joe whispered.

"She looks kind of familiar," Natalie said.

Frank got out the parabolic mike and put on a pair of headphones. He handed the other pair to Joe, who shared it with Natalie, then aimed the mike at Randall and the woman.

"Where's your partner?" they heard the woman say.

"He's coming," Randall said.

"You've had some good weather for jumping," the woman said.

"That's Janice Gainey, the reporter for the

Real Deal TV show," Natalie whispered excitedly to the Hardys. "I recognize the voice."

Frank and Joe nodded as they listened to Silk. "I didn't come out here to talk about the weather," he said. "Did you bring something for us?"

"Two hundred thousand is a lot of money, Randall," Janice Gainey said. "Since you screwed up on the Waller fall, I'm only authorized to give you the money after I've seen usable tape. Do you have it with you?"

"We're working on it."

"Just so we understand each other. It's only worth the two hundred grand if it clearly shows them . . . you know, hit the ground."

"Like I said, we're going to make it happen," Silk said.

Joe looked at Frank and Natalie. "They're going to stage an accident. They're filming it and selling it to—"

"Ssshhh!" Natalie hissed. They all listened.

"We're jumping at the Palisades near where the amusement park used to be," Silk said. "We've got the chutes rigged and—"

Janice Gainey cut him off. "I don't want any of the details. Just get me the tape."

Joe whipped off his headphones. "I'm going to go call Bob Edgewater and let him know what's going down."

"Good idea," Frank said. "We'll stay here and keep listening."

Joe moved as quickly and quietly as possible through the woods. He hopped into the van, picked up the cell phone, and dialed Edgewater's number. His assistant answered.

"Shirley, this is Joe Hardy. Can I speak to Mr. Edgewater, please? Fast."

"I'm afraid he's unavailable right now. If you care to—"

"It's an emergency," Joe said. "A life-and-death situation."

"I'm sorry, Joe. Mr. Edgewater is out on an investigation, but I can page him for you."

"Okay, thanks," Joe said. "When he calls back, tell him there's a jump planned for sometime this afternoon from the site of the old Palisades amusement park."

"Got it," said the assistant.

"Tell him somebody's trying to stage a fatal accident."

"I'll page him right away, Joe. Top priority."

"Thanks." Joe hung up and jumped out of the van. He ran back to the spot where he had left Frank and Natalie, and what he saw brought him to an abrupt halt. The two of them were walking into the meadow with their hands clasped behind their heads.

A man, whose face Joe couldn't see, held a gun to their backs.

Chapter

13

JOE DUCKED behind a tree to avoid being spotted by the gunman. Before risking another peek, he waited until Frank and Natalie had been marched another twenty yards toward where Randall and Janice Gainey were waiting. This time he saw the gunman clearly: it was Tomcat Kritzer. Then Silk Randall also drew a gun.

Joe crept to where Frank and Natalie had left the parabolic mike. He put on the headphones and aimed the mike at the group. "Good thing I decided to check the perimeter," Kritzer said. "You never know what's going to fall out of the trees."

"Listen, I don't want to have anything more to do with this," Gainey said.

"You're already in it up to your neck," Randall said.

"To the tune of two hundred grand," Kritzer added.

"You'd better not have told anyone else about this arrangement," Gainey said.

"Don't worry," Kritzer said. "Only the three of us know."

"Make sure you don't botch it this time like that Metrocorp jump," Gainey said.

"I told you," Silk said, "your camera malfunctioned."

"Just get me the tape and I'll have your money for you." She began to back away. "And as far as anyone is concerned, I was never here." She turned and walked away.

All of a sudden Joe realized that he and Frank were the targets for Silk's next rigged jump—a jump that was meant to be terminal. But now Silk had Natalie in place of Joe. He couldn't believe anyone could come up with such a demented scheme, just for money.

Joe considered creating a diversion, which might buy Frank enough time to overpower a single gunman. But with two armed men, Frank's chances were very slim. And Joe knew it would be impossible to convince the local police that such a wild story was true, so he figured his only real option was to get Squirrel, Shima, and the others to help.

Joe watched Kritzer and Randall force Frank

and Natalie into the yellow van, then drive away. Picking up the parabolic mike, he ran to his van and took off for the Ridgeway airport. He tried reaching Squirrel or the others at the Wild Blue Yonder on the van's cellular phone, but there was no answer, so all he could do was leave urgent messages.

When he got to Ridgeway Municipal, he pulled up in front of the jump school and ran inside. Several novice jumpers were in the classroom watching a slick promotional video of the operation.

"Has anyone seen Wayne Darcy around?" he said.

A middle-aged woman with salt-and-pepper hair asked, "Is that the jump supervisor?"

"Yes."

"He's taking a group up now," she replied.

"Thanks," Joe said as he ran back outside.

"I think they already took off," the woman shouted after him.

Joe jumped into the van and drove through a gate marked Authorized Vehicles Only. He saw the Wild Blue Yonder Twin Otter idling at the end of the runway, ready to take off. Joe floored the accelerator and aimed directly for the plane, flashing his headlights and honking his horn. The Twin Otter surged forward, quickly picking up speed.

Joe floored it and swerved so the van was running just ahead of the plane. When Darcy saw him, he eased back on the plane's throttle, bringing it to a stop at the edge of the runway. Joe hopped out and ran around to the Twin Otter's jump door. A scowling Wayne Darcy stood in the door, Squirrel and Dave Shima behind him.

Darcy jumped to the ground. "What kind of stunt was that, Hardy?" he yelled.

"Hold it," Joe said. "I can explain."

"If you were in the service I'd have you thrown in the brig." The veins in Darcy's forehead were bulging. "But since you're not, I'll personally see to it that you never jump again."

"Listen to me!" Joe shouted over the drone of the plane. "This is an emergency!"

"It had better be," Darcy grumbled. The jumpers piled out of the plane and gathered around.

"Silk and Tomcat took my brother and Nat at gunpoint. They're going to force them to do a BASE jump using chutes rigged not to open."

Darcy gave Joe an incredulous look. "You expect us to believe such a ridiculous story? You ought to have your head examined."

"I'm telling the truth," Joe said. He felt like screaming at them all in frustration, but he knew he had to keep a cool head. "If we don't get over to the Palisades right now, Nat and Frank are dead."

"Why would they do something like that?" Squirrel said. "It doesn't make any sense."

"Janice Gainey offered them two hundred

thousand for the videotape," Joe said, "as long as it shows someone hitting the ground."

"So why did they pick Frank and Nat?" Shima asked.

"It's a long story, but I'll give you the short version. Frank and I are investigators looking into Kurt Waller's death. That's why we joined your group. One thing led to another and we began to suspect Silk. We trailed him to a meeting with Janice Gainey, and when I left to call for backup, Tomcat showed up and found Frank and Nat spying on them."

"What was Nat doing there?" Squirrel asked.

"She stowed away in our van. Look, none of this matters right now. What we have to do is stop them from killing Frank and Nat. You've got to help me."

"This is nuts," Squirrel said.

"Look," Joe said, "I'm working with the FAA, and I've already got enough on all of you not only to ground you for good, but to have you thrown in jail. So forget about how unbelievable the story is. If you ever want to jump again, you're coming with me."

"All right, I'm with you," Shima said. "Guys?" He turned to Rush and Kamikaze, who both nodded.

"Count me in," Squirrel said.

Joe said, "Everybody in the van. We don't have a second to lose."

Shima, Rush, Kamikaze, and Darcy piled into

the back of the Hardys' van. Joe hopped in behind the wheel and Squirrel rode shotgun. Joe drove off the runway at top speed and headed for the expressway. With his foot to the floor, he darted in and out of slower traffic.

Wayne Darcy leaned nervously over the front seat. "I know we're in a hurry, but the state troopers are going to pull you over, Joe. That'll only slow us down."

"I hope they do," Joe said, swerving around a large semi. "That way we'd get a police escort."

"The only escort we'd get would be to jail. They'd never believe your story."

"You're probably right," Joe said, heading for the Cross Bronx Expressway and the George Washington Bridge. "But we don't have a choice." Joe didn't ease up on the accelerator.

"I haven't had this much fun since we jumped off the Chrysler Building," Squirrel said with a big grin on his face.

Darcy looked at him. "That was you?"

Squirrel slunk down in his seat. "Uh, yeah," he mumbled.

"You're not going to bust us, are you?" Rush asked.

"We'll discuss that later," Darcy said. "Right now we've got a more serious situation."

"Joe," Shima said. "What made you suspect Silk?"

Joe kept weaving around slow-moving vehicles as he explained. "Frank noticed this little black box in his helmet. We didn't know what it was, so we had a friend check it out. It turned out to be a tiny video camera."

"You're kidding," Squirrel said. "When I asked him about that he told me it was a new kind of altimeter."

"That must be why he always wanted a clear view of us," Kamikaze said. "He needed to get good shots of each of us landing."

"Or crashing," Rush added.

Traffic began to slow as they crossed over the Harlem River and into Manhattan.

"Silk and Kritzer were all set to sell Janice Gainey the tape of Kurt's last jump," Joe said, "but the camera didn't work right." He glanced back at the other jumpers. "Do any of you know what really happened that night?"

They shook their heads.

"We just figured Kurt made a turn, couldn't pull out, and lost it," Squirrel said.

They came to a dead stop in traffic. Joe banged his hand on the steering wheel and honked the horn in desperation. He could just see the top of the bridge over some buildings up ahead.

"There must be an accident," Darcy said.

Joe tuned the radio to an all-news station. After a report from Eastern Europe, a female traffic reporter came on the air.

"We're over the toll plaza on the New Jersey side of the George Washington Bridge where a jackknifed semi is blocking all westbound lanes," the reporter said. "Traffic is blocked up clear past the bridge into New York City. We're suggesting you find an alternate route or expect major delays. This is Tanya Gunther reporting from the All News TraffiCopter. Back to the studio."

Joe flicked off the radio in disgust and glanced at his watch. "We're running out of time."

"What do we do now?" Squirrel said.

Joe looked around behind them. "Hold on to your seats," he said. He drove the van up onto the curb so that the two tires on the right were riding it, while the left side was on the street. At this crazy angle he started passing cars. There was barely enough room for the van to squeeze between the line of cars and the guardrail. Angry motorists honked and shouted as Joe went past.

Joe made it less than halfway across the bridge before he came up to a line of cars that was blocking the curb. He leaned on the horn in frustration.

"We're stuck," Joe said grimly. "Frank's and Natalie's lives are at stake, and our luck just ran out."

Chapter

14

"WE MIGHT AS WELL just get out the binoculars and watch Nat and Frank crash from right here," Rush said. He and everyone else in the van were rapidly losing hope.

Joe tapped his thumb on the steering wheel as he stared across the river at the sheer cliffs of the Palisades. "Anybody know how far we are from the old amusement park?"

"I'd guess a good two miles," Squirrel said.

"All right, grab your equipment and let's go," Joe said.

"You can't leave the van here in the middle of the bridge," Kamikaze said.

"Oh, yeah?" Joe said. "Just watch me." He turned to the others. "Who's coming?"

137

"Let's do it," Squirrel shouted. Shima, Rush, Kamikaze, and Darcy grabbed their gear and bolted out of the van along with Squirrel and Joe. Single file, they started running between the lines of stalled cars toward New Jersey.

Meanwhile, Frank and Natalie sat on the floor in the back of Silk Randall's van, their hands tied behind their backs. Randall was at the wheel and Kritzer was in the front passenger seat.

"So what are you going to do after all this, Silk?" Kritzer asked.

"I'm going around the world BASE jumping," Silk said. "I'm going to do some extreme stuff—like that guy from Japan who climbed up Mt. Everest, skied down at a hundred miles an hour, then flew off a cliff and parasailed the rest of the way. How about you?"

"Yeah, let's hear it, Kritzer," Natalie said sarcastically.

"Why don't you two shut up back there?" Silk said.

Kritzer just turned and threw a dirty look at Frank and Natalie, who were trying to keep from falling over as the van went around a sharp curve. "I'm going to lie low and develop the business," he said to Silk. "Maybe upgrade one of the planes."

"Gee, you sure know how to have a good time," Silk said.

Kritzer stared at Silk. "You don't get it, do you?"

"Get what?" Silk asked.

"Life isn't just about going jumping all day long."

"So what's it about, Kritzer?" Natalie said. "Destroying people's livelihoods, killing people, just to make a lot of money?"

Silk suddenly hit the brakes and everyone lurched forward. Furious, he set the parking brake and turned around. "I told you two to shut up!" he screamed.

He started to climb into the back of the van. Kritzer grabbed him and shoved him back into his seat, growling, "Just calm down and drive."

Silk released the parking brake and drove on.

"When you get an opportunity, you have to seize it," Kritzer said. "Otherwise the competition will walk all over you."

Meanwhile Frank was looking for a way out. For the time being the best they could do was try to keep Kritzer and Silk distracted. "Is that why you did everything you could to make Spencer Johnson look bad?" he asked Kritzer.

"That old bum only got what he deserved," Kritzer said. "If I hadn't shut him down, somebody else would have."

"How can you talk like that?" Natalie said. "Spencer treated you like a son. And all you ever did was take, take, take. You're nothing but slime."

"Spencer's better off now," Kritzer said. "He couldn't take the stress anymore. And watch your mouth, miss."

Natalie went on. "He wouldn't have had that heart attack if it wasn't for you. If Spencer dies, it'll be your fault because you squeezed the life out of him. That'll be one more death on your hands."

Silk pulled off the road and brought the van to a stop. "You're not going to have to worry about that much longer," he said to Natalie. "We're at the end of the line."

Kritzer hopped out and opened the sliding door. He reached in and pulled Natalie and Frank out of the van. They were in a lot next to the old amusement park, which was deserted. Weeds grew tall where the giant roller coaster and concessions had once stood.

Silk took an equipment bag out of the van. Kritzer prodded Frank and Natalie past a stand of trees and along a path. A minute later they came out in a clearing with a view of the Hudson. Frank looked downriver at the George Washington Bridge and the skyline of Manhattan beyond.

While Kritzer trained his gun on Frank and Natalie, Silk cut their hands loose.

"Here," Silk said, pulling a helmet, harness, and parachute out of the duffel bag and handing them to Natalie. "Get into these."

When he reached into the bag again Frank was ready. He spun in the air and caught Silk in the head with a perfectly placed karate kick. Silk hit the ground hard, and Frank was standing over him in a flash, ready to hit him again.

"Stop right there, Hardy." Frank looked up to see Kritzer pointing his gun at Natalie. Frank had no choice but to back away from Silk, who got to his feet, obviously still stunned from the blow. He shoved a helmet as hard as he could into Frank's stomach, then dropped a parachute and harness at Frank's feet and said, "Put them on *now*. They're all set for your jump, punk." He turned toward Natalie. "Same goes for you."

"What makes you think you're going to get away with this?" Natalie said as she wriggled into the harness.

"It worked with Kurt Waller, didn't it?"

"Did it?" Frank asked. "I happen to know the FAA hasn't closed the file on Kurt's death yet."

"Why wouldn't they?" Kritzer said. "There's no evidence it was anything but an unfortunate accident."

"The agency doesn't see it that way." Frank was playing for time, hoping Joe had been able to reach Edgewater. "And they won't believe this was an accident either."

"That's enough chatter," Kritzer said. He waved his gun at Frank and Natalie. "Put on those helmets and step over to the edge."

They did as they were told. Frank looked down the sheer face of the Palisades to the rocks and the water below. The wind swirled up off the river in gusts that made it hard to stand still.

"It's five hundred feet to the bottom," Kritzer said. "Even for an experienced BASE jumper, it's not an easy location. And with these winds your accidents will be quite believable."

"If you jump out far enough you might miss the rocks," Silk added. "But come to think of it, from this height the water will be just as fatal."

He had a weird smile on his face. It occurred to Frank that Silk was actually enjoying himself.

"I take it you're the one who's going to cover the jump with that miniature camera inside your helmet," Frank said.

Silk tried to hide his surprise. "Who told you about that?"

"I noticed it during the bridge jump," Frank said. "Joe and I borrowed the helmet from your locker and had it checked out. That's a pricey little piece of equipment. We also know you got it from *The Real Deal.*"

Silk slipped into his harness, igoring Frank.

"There are a few things you obviously haven't considered," Frank continued.

"Like what?" Silk asked.

"What are you going to do about Joe, for instance? He knows everything I know about your plan. And he's told the FAA by now. He was with us when we were listening in on your little conversation with Janice Gainey at the park. He left to make a call from our van. They're probably on their way right now."

"Nice try," Kritzer said.

"Hey, what if he's telling the truth?" Silk said, a tinge of panic creeping into his voice.

"Think about it," Natalie said. "You're going to be charged with murder."

Kritzer smiled. "They're bluffing. Besides, Silk, you'll be thousands of miles away by then and filthy rich."

While Silk was focused on Kritzer, Frank clamped down on the jumper's hand and forced his gun toward the ground. Silk and Frank struggled, and Frank almost had control of the gun when Kritzer shouted, "Back off or I shoot her."

Frank looked up to see Kritzer holding his gun to Natalie's temple.

"What good does that do you?" Frank said. "And if you think I'm just going to step off the cliff for you, you're dead wrong. You're going to have to shoot me, too, and nobody's going to believe Nat and I had an accident when they pry bullets out of us."

"He's right," Silk said. "This is all going wrong."

"Shut up, Silk," Kritzer said. "Just stick to the plan and everything will be okay. Is the camera ready?"

Silk put on his helmet, his gun still trained on Frank. "We're rolling."

"Good," Kritzer said. "You'll cover the first

fall from up here, then fly down and catch the other from below. Got it?"

Silk nodded. Kritzer prodded Natalie right to the edge of the cliff. Frank was about to rush Kritzer, who still had his gun pointed at Natalie. Frank figured he had nothing left to lose and that he'd go out fighting. But just then he heard the rustle of footsteps coming from the trees. They turned to see Joe, Squirrel, and the other jumpers, all wearing their skydiving gear, burst into the clearing.

"Hold it right there!" Joe shouted.

"No, you hold it," Kritzer said. He had Natalie by the shoulders. Joe and the others took a step forward.

"Don't move," Kritzer said. "Any of you. She's going over. And nobody's going to stop it."

Silk trained his gun on Joe and the jumpers. "I'm ready when you are," he said to Kritzer.

Natalie started struggling with Kritzer at the edge. She dug her heels into the ground and clawed at his face with her fingers. But Kritzer wrapped his powerful arms around her, picked her up, and threw her.

"Aaaahhhh!" she screamed as she went over the edge.

Chapter

15

THEN EVERYTHING happened at once.

The second Kritzer threw Natalie over, Joe took a running leap into the air after her.

Silk was so intent on following Natalie's fall with his camera helmet that Frank broke away from him and tackled Kritzer near the edge of the cliff. They hit the ground rolling, Frank struggling to hold Kritzer's gun hand at arm's length. The two of them rolled to within inches of the edge. Kritzer brought the muzzle of the gun down until it was aimed directly at Frank's face. Frank pushed the gun away just before he fired, and the bullet went into the ground.

Kritzer fired again, but all Frank heard was a click. Then Kritzer hit him in the head with the gun butt, dazing him momentarily and knocking him over the edge. He grabbed onto a small tree growing out of the rock, his legs dangling in space.

Meanwhile, Joe caught Natalie in midair. He wrapped one hand around her waist and pulled his rip cord with the other. The chute opened, slowing their fall, and he clipped his harness to hers. Then a strong gust of wind pushed them back toward the cliff.

"Bank left," Natalie yelled.

Trying to steer, Joe pulled on the lines, but he couldn't get a sense of the swirling wind. He kept pulling hard, but they were still headed for the cliff. Finally they began to turn. Natalie's feet grazed the rock face as they carved a slow arc out over the water.

Natalie looked down and pointed. "There's a good spot over there," she shouted. "Go for it."

"I'll do my best," Joe said.

Joe fought another gust and tried to guide them to the spot, but they were sinking too fast. They swooped down and Joe could see the icy waters of the Hudson rushing up to meet them. A split second later they went in feet first with a huge splash.

At the top of the Palisades, Shima, Rush, and Kamikaze swarmed over Silk and wrestled him down. Squirrel saw Kritzer leap off the cliff, and he dived after him.

"Go get him, Squirrel!" Frank yelled, still hanging on to the small tree on the rock face.

Frank watched Squirrel grab Kritzer from behind and pull his rip cord. But Kritzer broke free when Squirrel's chute snapped open and waited till the last possible moment to pop his chute.

Seconds later Frank saw Kritzer land hard on the ground right next to the water. He got to his feet and quickly began to wriggle out of his harness. He was fighting the wind for control of his chute. Kritzer finally dropped the harness, but Squirrel was right on his tail. Squirrel came crashing into Kritzer and knocked him to the ground as he landed on top of him.

Natalie and Joe struggled up from under Joe's chute, swam to shore, and climbed out of the frigid water onto the rocky embankment. Joe saw Kritzer stagger to his feet and go after Squirrel, who was wrestling with his chute. Joe spun Kritzer around and caught him in the jaw with a sharp right uppercut. The jump school owner went down like a sack of potatoes and didn't get up.

At the top of the cliff the tree Frank was holding on to began tearing away at the roots. "Hey," he yelled, "somebody give me a hand down here."

Darcy ran to Frank. He whipped off his flight jacket, wrapped one sleeve around his wrist, and lowered the other sleeve down to Frank. "Grab on, and I'll pull you up," he shouted.

147

Frank let go of the tree with one hand and took hold of the rope just as the tree's roots ripped away from the edge of the cliff. Kamikaze and Rush reached over the edge and helped pull Frank to the top.

Down below, Joe, Natalie, and Squirrel tied Kritzer's hands behind his back using line from one of the parachutes. They marched their captive along the base of the Palisades until they found a steep path that led to the top in a series of switchbacks. Up top, Natalie kept the gun Kritzer had dropped trained on Silk while Frank pulled the helmet with the miniature camera off Silk's head and tucked it under his arm.

The sound of sirens in the distance grew until three local squad cars followed by an unmarked car screeched into the parking lot. Bob Edgewater got out of the unmarked car and trotted over to Natalie.

"I'm Natalie Hernandez from the Johnson Jump Academy, and I think these are the guys you're looking for," Natalie said. She still had the gun pointed at Silk and Kritzer.

"Good work," Edgewater said, nodding to several uniformed police officers, who led the suspects to the squad cars. He looked around. "Where are the Hardys?"

"Right here." Joe's voice came from under the yellow van. He crawled out holding a metal box

148

the size of a dictionary, followed by Frank. They were both covered with dirt and grease.

"I came as soon as I got your message, Joe," Edgewater said. He looked at the metal box. "What's that?"

"All the evidence you need for a conviction," Joe said. He handed it to the FAA investigator.

"It's a videotape recorder," Frank added. "They recorded all their jumps with a remote minicamera." He turned Silk's helmet over to Edgewater.

"Outstanding," Edgewater said. "It's not every day I have an entire case handed to me on a silver platter." He hefted the recorder in both hands, then looked down at the smudges it left. "Or in this case a dirty black box."

Everyone chuckled, then turned to congratulate the Hardys on a job well done.

Joe was about to shake Edgewater's hand when he saw that his own hand had mud and grease on it from being under the van.

"What's a little dirt?" Edgewater said, taking his hand.

"It's just fine with me," Joe said. "I'll never complain about crawling in dirt as long as I live."

"Right," Frank added. "Anything to remain on the ground instead of flying in the air again."

Frank and Joe's next case:

Frank and Joe have come to Germany to assist archaeologist Dr. John Maxwell in his search for a legendary jewel-encrusted shield. The priceless artifact is rumored to be buried in the lost ruins of an ancient Roman fortress. But the boys discover more than the shield is missing: Maxwell himself has vanished without a trace! Hunting for both Maxwell and the shield, the Hardys make some powerful, ruthless enemies. From vicious attack dogs to armor-clad thugs, they face a new fight at every turn. But as they descend into a labyrinth of lies, Frank and Joe are determined to unearth the truth—no matter how deep, dark, and deadly it is . . . in *The Emperor's Shield,* Case #119 in The Hardy Boys Casefiles™.

Christopher Pike presents....
a frighteningly fun new series for your younger brothers and sisters!

The Secret Path 53725-3/$3.50
The Howling Ghost 53726-1/$3.50
The Haunted Cave 53727-X/$3.50
Aliens in the Sky 53728-8/$3.99
The Cold People 55064-0/$3.99
The Witch's Revenge 55065-9/$3.99
The Dark Corner 55066-7/$3.99
The Little People 55067-5/$3.99
The Wishing Stone 55068-3/$3.99
The Wicked Cat 55069-1/$3.99
The Deadly Past 55072-1/$3.99
The Hidden Beast 55073-X/$3.99
The Creature in the Teacher
00261-9/$3.99
The Evil House 00262-7/$3.99

A MINSTREL® BOOK

Now your younger brothers or sisters
can take a walk down Fear Street....

R·L·STINE'S

GHOSTS OF FEAR STREET ®

1 Hide and Shriek   52941-2/$3.99
2 Who's Been Sleeping in My Grave? 52942-0/$3.99
3 Attack of the Aqua Apes   52943-9/$3.99
4 Nightmare in 3-D   52944-7/$3.99
5 Stay Away From the Tree House   52945-5/$3.99
6 Eye of the Fortuneteller   52946-3/$3.99
7 Fright Knight   52947-1/$3.99
8 The Ooze   52948-X/$3.99
9 Revenge of the Shadow People   52949-8/$3.99
10 The Bugman Lives   52950-1/$3.99
11 The Boy Who Ate Fear Street   00183-3/$3.99
12 Night of the Werecat   00184-1/$3.99
13 How to be a Vampire   00185-X/$3.99
14 Body Switchers from Outer Space
                                                         00186-8/$3.99
15 Fright Christmas   00187-6/$3.99

A MINSTREL BOOK

Simon & Schuster Mail Order
200 Old Tappan Rd., Old Tappan, N.J. 07675
Please send me the books I have checked above. I am enclosing $_____ (please add
$0.75 to cover the postage and handling for each order. Please add appropriate sales
tax). Send check or money order—no cash or C.O.D.'s please. Allow up to six weeks
for delivery. For purchase over $10.00 you may use VISA: card number, expiration
date and customer signature must be included.

POCKET
BOOKS

Name _____

Address _____

City _____ State/Zip _____

VISA Card # _____ Exp.Date _____

Signature _____
                                                                    1180-11